MVFOL

Dear Mystery Lover,

One of the pleasures of being the editor of DEAD LET-TER is the chance to work with my colleagues at St. Martin's Press to find fresh new voices in the mystery genre and to coordinate individual publishing programs for each of our hard/soft authors. Candace M. Robb, Manuel Ramos, Marian Babson, J. S. Borthwick, Peter Bowen, Graham Landrum, Kathryn Buckstaff, S. J. Rozan, Susan Holtzer, Ann Dukthas, James Bradberry, Laura Crum, Ian Morson, and Elliott Roosevelt are all St. Martin's hardcover and DEAD LETTER paperback authors.

St. Martin's is the leader in publishing first novelists, especially first mystery novelists, and I am pleased to introduce the newest addition to our growing hard/soft list, Wendi Lee.

*The Good Daughter* is Wendi's first mystery novel and Angela Matelli's first big case. Born and raised in East Boston, MA, Angela returns to her hometown after a stint in the U.S. Marine Corps to set up shop as a private investigator. With a tough and sexy protagonist and the wonderful Boston setting, Wendi continues in the female private investigator tradition of Sara Paretsky, Sue Grafton, and Boston's other female P.I. writer, Linda Barnes.

Keep your eye out for DEAD LETTER—and build yourself a library of paperback mysteries to die for.

Yours in crime,

Shawn Coyne
Senior Editor
St. Martin's DEAD

D0957252

# The Good Daughter

*An Angela Matelli Mystery*

## WENDI LEE

St. Martin's Paperbacks

THE GOOD DAUGHTER

Copyright © 1994 by Wendi Lee.

Library of Congress Catalog Card Number: 94-19662

ISBN: 0-312-95696-7

Printed in the United States of America

St. Martin's Press hardcover edition/ November 1994
St. Martin's Paperbacks edition/ January 1996

10  9  8  7  6  5  4  3  2  1

*For my mother*
*Bette Carlson Merslich*
*With love*

# Acknowledgments

I have the following people to thank for their contributions, input, and support: Keith Kahla, Barbara Puechner, Kate Stine, Mari Famulari, Lynn Whitacre, Rick Noel, Jurgen Stroda, Max Allan Collins, Ed Gorman, Barbara Collins, Kim Fryer, Bob Randisi, Debra Sorenson, Boston private investigator Jack O'Malley, Andria at the Boston Chamber of Commerce, Teresa Sisemore, Kathy Ptacek, Gaby Pauer, and the Writers on the Avenue. And many thanks to my husband, Terry Beatty, for always being my first editor.

# ♣ Chapter 1

*I* slowed down when I noticed the dead body. It was lying on the ground near the Haymarket Subway Station, a Suffolk County meat wagon was parked at a discreet distance, and a cop was trying to hold back all of us rubbernecking pedestrians. But let's face it—a corpse during Monday morning rush hour is as close to excitement as most people get all week.

The cop was big and beefy. All cops in Boston are big and beefy. And Irish. At least, that's always been my experience.

I caught a glimpse of the victim's face just before the attendants turned him over onto their portable gurney. He had that look of surprise mugging victims get when they realize that it really hurts to be knifed and maybe they won't live to tell about it after all.

The officer in charge of crowd control noticed me lurking on the edge of the crime scene and immediately walked up, his arms spread wide as if to block my view.

"All right, now, miss," he said in his best officious tone, "move along. There's nothing to see."

"What happened to him?" I asked.

The cop smiled back, businesslike and patronizing,

and replied, "Nothing for you to worry about, miss. Some man got himself mugged and knifed."

A man standing next to me nudged my arm and said, "Pretty exciting stuff, huh?" He made me feel like a ghoul, standing there watching the paramedics load the stretcher into the ambulance. I scowled at him before turning away from the scene, then walked briskly the rest of the way to my office, which was located in the North End, the trendy Italian section of Boston. Although it was late by most working people's standards, I'm a private investigator with my own office hours and ten o'clock in the morning was early enough for me. Of course, this was my first day in the PI business.

I have a nice little office—and *little* is the operative word. It's a twelve-by-twelve cubicle on the second floor of a brownstone owned by my mother's sorority sister's husband. I got a deal on the rent because my mother and Aunt Eloise, as I called her, were as close as Siamese twins. Against his wishes, Uncle Harry (who hates it when I call him that) was nagged into giving me a space in a prime business location for half of what anyone else would have paid. When I signed the check for the first and last month's rent plus a security deposit and handed it over, Uncle Harry flashed me a toothy smile, but his ears were red with irritation, probably at the idea of receiving half the rent he could have gotten. He snatched the check from my lily-white hand and as he pocketed it, said, "Nice doing business with you, Angie." Must have been hard to say through gritted teeth.

I had to climb the stairs—the elevator was out of order—but it was a beautiful sight to see my name painted on the pebbled glass door in sturdy black letters: ANGELA MATELLI, PRIVATE INVESTIGATOR.

I opened the door and stepped into the gloomy room, brightening it by pulling a grimy string that switched on the twenty-watt bulb in the ceiling light fixture. I had managed to squeeze quite a bit into such a small space—a big old oak file, two chairs, a small couch (in case a client faints), and my office desk, which sat in the center of the room like a smug Buddha.

Reaching into my large shoulder bag, I withdrew my recent purchases, a .40 Star and accompanying pants holster. The holster was made of lightweight nylon web fabric and clipped to the waistband at the small of my back. After fitting the Star into the holster, I tried it on for size and comfort. Although I could feel it back there, I was more comfortable with the Star than the .45 sidearm that had been the military standard issue for years. That had come with a lovely belt holster made of leather that chafed when I walked. I took the Star out and hoisted it, feeling the weight of stainless steel casing and vulcanized rubber grip. It had been drilled into me for eight years that drawing a gun meant I'd better be prepared to use it. Not that I expected to use it much, but I was more comfortable having one available.

Still, I had no illusions about the private eye business. I'd read a few detective novels and had really enjoyed them, but my reasons for being in the investigation field had more to do with my limited job skills than with romantic fantasies involving tough guys with names like Spade, Marlowe, or Hammer. I doubted my caseload would involve anything more demanding or dangerous than trailing an unfaithful spouse.

When I graduated from high school in the late seventies, my choices were college or secretarial school. I entered the university only to find myself changing my major every semester, depending on which professor fascinated me at the moment. After two years, I got restless. Since I had no aptitude for typing and I couldn't see spending another two or more years confined to classes, I joined the Marine Corps.

Back in the early eighties, the Marines weren't particularly looking for a few good women unless those women had clerical skills. They didn't know what else to do with us. But I signed on for two years with the hope that I might discover what I was good at. When I told my mother what I'd done, she almost had a heart attack. So did most of my fellow Marines. But I stuck with it and after I went through basic training on Parris Island in South Carolina, I was given a battery of aptitude tests to find out what I was best suited to do in the armed forces.

Since most of the female recruits ended up as typists and clerks, they stuck me behind a desk. But my hunt-and-peck method of typing and my careless filing habits irritated the sergeant I was assigned to, so I became his driver. Like I said, back then they didn't know what to do with us women in the Marines. After about a year of that, I was transferred to the military police.

I did well there and eventually ended up with the Special Investigations Division. I signed on for six more years and by the end of my stint, I had worked my way up to staff sergeant in undercover operations, mostly in Japan. I knew I could never make a lifetime commitment to the military, so while I was still in my twenties, I was anxious to adjust to civilian life. The last three months I spent in the military were probably the hardest for me. I knew I was leaving behind both good friends and a steady income for a crazy family and an unreliable job market. With my military background, I knew that I would probably be accepted into the Boston Police Department immediately, or that some big security or investigation firm would offer me my own desk. But I was tired of everyone telling me what to do. I wanted to be my own boss. So I became a private investigator.

I debated whether to keep the gun in my office or at home, or carry it with me everywhere I went. After weighing my choices, I had decided that I would feel a little too much like a gunfighter in the Old West if I carried it with me at all times. I had a baseball bat at home, in case I ran into an intruder. I would most likely need a gun here in the office when I went out on cases. Opening the bottom left-hand drawer, I slipped the holstered gun in carefully, locking the drawer and depositing the key in my pants pocket.

I sat behind my battle-scarred desk, testing the swivel in my ancient office chair. It groaned when I leaned back, so I carefully straightened up and looked at the basic black push-button multi-line office phone and answering machine which sat solidly on my desktop to the right. None of the buttons were lit up, but I hadn't been expecting any calls yet. I checked my answering machine for calls—there were none—then turned it off. I sighed and picked up the Boston *Globe* I'd bought at the corner store, thumbing through it in search of the small ad I had placed the other day.

The phone rang. I jumped, and almost fell backward out of my chair. After righting myself, balance being one of the things I learned in the Marine Corps, I answered it.

"Angela Matelli here," I said crisply.

"Hiya darling," a familiar voice drawled.

"Ma," I whined. I felt this immediate, cloying sense of guilt, like a schoolkid who'd been caught playing hooky. Come to think of it, I had played hooky in high school and never been caught. I guess maybe these things catch up with you eventually.

"Ma," I said again, "what are you doin' calling here? This is my business phone. I can't have relatives calling me during business hours."

"This is your first day, Angela," Ma reminded me, like

I needed reminding. "I wanted to find out how things are going."

"Well, I just got into the office and the phone's not exactly ringing off the hook yet." I tried to sound brave, but my voice wavered. I was disgusted with myself. "I'm going to put out some feelers."

"Your ad's in today's paper," she pointed out. "I'll cut it out so you can save it."

"Yeah, thanks, Ma," I said absently. What the heck did she think I was going to do with my ad—put it in a scrapbook? But that's probably exactly what she expected me to do.

". . . so he'll be dropping by today," she was saying.

I came back to reality and said, "Hey, wait. Run that by me again, Ma."

She sighed. "Honestly, Angela. I don't know how you made it through eight years in the Marines as a private detective."

"Criminal investigator, Ma. Now I'm a private detective. Repeat what you just said a moment ago. Please."

"I said that Uncle Charlie's friend will be stopping by today. He wants to hire you for something."

I blinked and perked up. " 'No-Legs' Charlie?"

Ma was silent for a moment, then said, "I hate it when you call him that, Angela. Please have a little more respect for your elders. I thought the Marines would have at least taught you respect."

Now it was my turn to sigh. "Right, Ma. Uncle Charlie. What about his friend?"

"His name is Mr. Grady and he was on the force with your uncle many years ago."

Uncle Charlie had been a cop before he lost his legs, probably the only Italian cop in Boston. Of course, that's not entirely true, but it certainly seemed that way to me. He was the one who helped me get my license. Just before

I finished my military stint, he sent me the forms to fill out. I then sent the application and fee in to the Bureau of Special Licenses. Uncle Charlie boasted about how he made a few calls to the right places and got my paperwork pushed through within a few weeks. I later found out that it only takes two to three weeks to get your license if your record is clean with the state police. Still, I had my private investigator's license and I graciously thanked my uncle, leaving out that fact.

After Uncle Charlie retired, he got diabetes and didn't do anything about it for a long time. He hated doctors, so it wasn't until he was at death's door that they wheeled him into Brigham Memorial Hospital. And as a result, they had to operate.

But after he recovered and went into physical therapy, Uncle Charlie got around in his wheelchair and was as cheerful as could be. In fact, he was even more socially active nowadays than before he went into the hospital. My uncle actually insisted that we call him "No-Legs" Charlie, and it stuck.

"Does Mr. Grady have a first name, Ma?"

"Thomas."

"Do you have any idea what his problem is?"

I was hoping it wasn't a divorce case. I wasn't above sneaking around sleazy motels and snapping souvenirs of the occasion, but I was hoping that my first case wouldn't involve slipping fins into the sweating palms of motel clerks just to get a peek at the register. To avoid taking on too many divorce cases, I was planning to hit a few repo and insurance agencies in the area and working out a deal with them to take on some of their freelance work like credit checks and investigating insurance claims. That was the kind of excitement I planned on to make my daily bread.

Ma was talking and I tuned in again. "I'm not sure of

the specifics, but I think it has something to do with his daughter."

"I see."

There was some rustling noise in the background on Ma's end and she said, "Listen, darling. I got to go now. Your sister just got here with her two . . . kids."

I knew she wanted to say "brats," but my sister Sophia was probably within earshot. I understood and said, "Well, don't let them get away with anything today. Lay down the law."

I knew, and Ma knew, that by the end of the day, those kids would be walking all over her. We said good-bye with promises to get together for dinner later in the week, and hung up.

It wasn't that Sophia's kids, Michael and Stephanie, were horrible. It was just that Sophia had gotten knocked up when she was still a kid herself and Dave, the father, left her soon after Stephanie was born. Although Dave had been ordered to pay child support, he took off for parts unknown and remained a deadbeat dad to this day. I think Sophia's situation reminded Ma of our father taking off when we were toddlers, so she felt guilty enough to allow Sophia to manipulate her into baby-sitting.

Sophia was a barfly. She worked as a cocktail waitress down at the Rusty Pelican, and her whole social life revolved around going to bars with her friends and picking up guys. She had a soft spot for bikers. We'd had quite a few arguments about her idea of recreation and social responsibility.

I shuddered to think about it. Maybe bars were okay back in the seventies, but not in this day and age. But Sophia had never had a chance to grow up and I guess this was her way of rebelling against the responsibility she'd been saddled with at such a young age.

The knock rattled the pebbled glass and made my

heart leap into my throat. First the phone, then the door. I had to calm down. I was pretty jumpy today, but then, I *did* walk past a dead guy about an hour ago, so maybe I had an excuse. I took a deep breath and said, "Come in, door's open."

A man in his mid-sixties stepped through the door. His florid face and compact body told me that although he might be retired, he kept himself in pretty good shape. His thick white hair and bushy white eyebrows were a startling contrast to his blue eyes. If he'd been twenty years younger, I'd have made a pass at him. Blue eyes make me weak in the knees.

I took another deep breath and nodded at the only other chair in the office, a straight-backed affair I'd picked up on the street the other day. Literally. People in Boston throw away the damnedest things.

My potential client sat down facing me from across my desk and extended his hand.

"I'm Tom Grady," he said. "Your uncle said he'd get word to you that I'd be stopping by."

Wow. Things were happening fast. I tried not to look overwhelmed.

"Actually, I just got off the phone with my mother," I explained, conscious of how childish that sounded. But Tom Grady just smiled. I continued, "She mentioned you, but not your problem. How can I help you, Mr. Grady?"

He cleared his throat. "Well, it's about my daughter Sheilah."

I nodded encouragingly, letting him tell it at his own pace.

When I didn't say anything, he launched into his explanation. "Well, she's moved in with this fellow, see. His name is Brian Scanlon. I don't trust him. And I'd like to have him followed, if you do that sort of thing."

Oh, boy. My first case would be just the sort I wasn't looking forward to: following some poor slob to work and back home, working around the clock, sipping coffee and blowing on my fingers when the temperature dropped below freezing at night. What kind of lousy job is that?

I said, "Let's have the details."

# ♣ Chapter 2

"What exactly do you suspect Sheilah's boyfriend of doing, Mr. Grady?" I asked.

He looked down at his hands, apparently turning the question around in his mind. Finally he said, "Actually, I don't have anything to go on. It's more of a feeling."

He must have read my skeptical expression. "Miss Matelli, I was on the force for thirty-five years," he explained. "I walked a beat most of the time. I got to be a good judge of character. Sometimes it was hard to tell the difference between the scum and the decent people, and I had to rely on my instincts. They've gotten to be pretty reliable. So I'm relying on them now."

His explanation sounded pretty good. Being a civilian cop wasn't all that different from being a military cop. Of course, we played by some very different rules, but one thing all law officers worth their salt have is good instinct.

Still, I felt that he was holding back some vital piece of information. Call it instinct.

I tried a different tactic. "Mr. Grady, you must still have connections down at your old precinct. Why don't you just have your friends check out this boyfriend?"

Tom Grady looked away and said, "I have my reasons

for keeping this private, the first and foremost being my daughter." He looked back at me and leaned forward. "If Sheilah ever found out that I'd checked up on her boyfriend, there'd be no livin' with her. She might even stop speaking to me. I'd like to avoid that if I can."

I knew this was a two-part answer, so I prompted him with, "What else?"

Grady looked sheepish. "I don't really know anyone on the force anymore. All the guys down there are young and sharp. College educated." He almost spat the last words out. Grady was one of the old cops, the guys who got the job because of their brawn rather than their brains. He rubbed the back of his neck and shook his head, adding, "It's just not the same gang anymore."

*Retirement is breaking up that old gang of mine,* I thought.

In a gentler tone, I asked, "Do you have anything else to go on, anything other than instinct?"

He compressed his mouth into a thin line and shook his head silently. I was sure there was something else. Maybe I was wrong, but I didn't think so.

I said, "Okay, I said earlier that I'd take the case. So how about giving me some data on this guy?"

My client sized me up, then said, "Before I give you any particulars, can I ask you a few questions first?"

"Ask away," I said in a breezy tone. Too bad my mood didn't match.

"Charlie said you were a Marine in the MP division. How long were you in the service?"

"Eight years," I replied.

"What rank did you leave with?"

"Staff sergeant. I worked in Special Investigations."

"Miss Matelli . . ." Tom Grady hesitated, then continued, "I just want you to know why I chose you. I want a woman investigator who can be tough if she gets into a tight spot."

I was curious, but I kept my expression impassive. "Why not a male investigator?"

"Because if Sheilah or Brian suspect that I've hired an investigator to check up on him, they'll most likely be looking for a man, not a woman. Sheilah thinks I'm a bit more old-fashioned than I really am . . . a male chauvinist, you know. Have you had any experience tailing suspects?"

I could have given him a flip answer like, *Gee, that's all I ever did in the Marines,* but I decided not to alienate my first client. Instead I said, "I've had some experience. When I was stationed in Japan, it was hard to tail another American soldier in Tokyo because we stuck out like sore thumbs. But I got pretty good at it."

What was running through my mind while I said this was, how would Sheilah and Brian find out that her father hired an investigator to check out the boyfriend's background unless Tom Grady inadvertently slipped them the information? If there's one thing I hate, it's the idea that I'm the cheese in the mousetrap. This cat-and-mouse game was starting to annoy me. I hated knowing that a client was withholding information that might prove vital.

"Mr. Grady . . ." I began, then decided to get more personal and more direct. "Tom. How are they going to find out unless you tell them?"

He turned red and shifted uncomfortably in his chair. It was clear from the look on his face that he knew he'd said too much. He changed the subject by giving me a recent picture of Sheilah and Brian, their work and home addresses, and the bare facts. Brian Scanlon was a longshoreman. Sheilah did the books for one of the shipping companies on the docks, Shamrock Imports. They met almost a year ago.

"How much do you charge per day?" He took out his checkbook and a pen.

I perked up, willing to completely forget the previous line of conversation in lieu of an income. While I wasn't going to forget Tom Grady's evasion by any means, I knew I would eventually discover what he wasn't willing to tell me. But I would have to find out the hard way.

After Tom Grady wrote out a check for three days' work plus expense money, he stood up, shook my hand, and left. I sat back in my chair and kissed the check. I'd deposit it in my checking account on my way home this afternoon. Meanwhile, I decided to forgo the obligatory background check on Brian Scanlon until tomorrow. I was anxious to start the surveillance from Scanlon's place of employment and follow him from there tonight.

Sheilah Grady and Brian Scanlon's home address was in Chelsea. This was convenient for me because I lived in the neighboring community of East Boston. I grew up in East Boston and went to school there. When I returned from my eight-year stint in the corps, I moved back to the only town I'd ever known and, through my complicated and accommodating Italian family, found and bought the apartment building that I currently lived in.

Generally speaking, Italian families are huge affairs that extend beyond brothers and sisters, aunts, uncles, and cousins. Italian families have adopted aunts and uncles, as in the case of my Aunt Eloise and Uncle Harry, and second cousins on your father's side and, well, the list goes on.

I left the office a little after twelve, had an eggplant parmesan sub and a cappuccino at one of the North End delis, then took the subway back home.

My apartment building is on Marginal Street, overlooking the Boston Harbor. East Boston is a small piece of land that juts out from the borders of Revere and Chelsea. There is no bridge that connects Boston to East Boston, but there is the tunnel. When I was a child, we had a choice of using the subway to get where we were going or, if Dad wanted to take the family into Boston "proper" for a day, we'd pile in the car and drive up to Revere, hang a left at Chelsea, then take the Mystic Bridge across through Charlestown. From there, we'd head down into Boston's North Station district where the Celtics used to hang other teams out to dry in the Boston Garden with the help of their vicious fans. The Celtics ain't been the same ever since the Lakers took the championship in Boston Garden a few years ago.

I was very lucky to get a building with a view. East Boston had been a well-kept secret until about a decade ago when the yuppies started buying up apartment buildings and turning them into upscale townhouses. They've been pushing the Italian community into Revere and other outlying areas for the past eight years.

Since my first day in boot camp, I'd been saving and investing my money. When I got out of the service, I was financially stable enough to buy some property, and Boston waterfront property was very choice.

Through my family connections, I found this place and made a bid. Fortunately for me at the time, the real estate market was in my favor—the prime rate was up and, as a result, there weren't many buyers. With my status as a vet, and my Uncle Sharkey (a real estate developer with the right connections), I was able to finagle a good finance deal. Of course, the building needed a bit of work, but that's where my lovely sister comes in. Not Sophia with the two brats, but my youngest sister, Rosa. She was living at home, attending the university out in Dorchester while working a part-time job, and not getting along with Ma.

Rosa and Ma had never gotten along very well, but it was tolerable when the rest of the family was around. When everyone had moved out and it was just Ma and Rosa, their fights escalated.

Fresh out of the Marines, I came back here, bought the building, moved into the third floor apartment, and offered one of the remaining two apartments to Rosa. She was thrilled and moved in the same week, with the understanding that she'd fix it up and act as manager of the third apartment, which has yet to be rented out. So far, it's been a good deal for us both.

I have several neighbors whose visiting friends look hungrily at my apartment building. I've even had a few offers to buy the property for far more than it's worth, but so far, no one's been able to put a price on my home turf.

There are four major subway lines—red, green, orange, and blue. The blue line runs all the way out to Wonderland in Revere, but I only took it as far as Maverick Square. My apartment building was only two blocks away, but on this cold day in early March, it seemed like two miles.

Rosa was home. She popped her head out the door when I'd climbed to the second-floor landing. People are always telling us that Rosa is a younger, smaller version of me. She has the same olive complexion, wavy dark hair, and brown eyes.

That's where the resemblance ends. Rosa wears her hair in a short punk cut and she has chipmunk cheeks, all of which make her look like a younger, ethnic Gidget.

I grinned at her and said, "Maybe I should put an elevator in here for my convenience."

"I thought Marine staff sergeants were made of sterner

stuff," she quipped. "Hey, Sarge, come on in and have a cold beer. You gotta see what I did to the living room."

I was going to tell her to lay off the "Sarge" routine, but the thought of a cold beer put the idea out of my mind. She ushered me in and, hands on her hips, surveyed her handiwork.

"Well, what do you think?"

The walls were painted lemon yellow with aqua trim. The furniture was comfortable—a folded turquoise futon for a couch, several director's chairs scattered around, boomerang-shaped coffee table. I remembered when we picked up the coffee table at a local thrift shop. Rosa fell in love with it the minute she laid eyes on it.

I sighed. "This is beautiful, Rosa. I wish I could get my apartment to have such a finished look."

She wrinkled her nose and said, "You've been in the Marines too long, Sarge. You're used to that spartan look. Once you've been a civilian for a while, you'll figure out what to do with your place."

She was right. My apartment looked like all the Marine digs I'd ever lived in. Olive drab and khaki were practically its only colors. I'd only been out of the service less than four months. I'd gotten used to buying everything at the PX for convenience's sake, and I'd been moved around so much that I hadn't had much time to soak up civilian life until I got my walking papers.

"So Ma tells me that you've got your first client lined up already," Rosa said.

I grimaced. Our mother sure got around. By now, I was certain that the whole family tree knew about it.

"Yeah. He came to see me about two hours ago," I replied. "His name's Tom Grady. Used to work with Uncle Charlie."

" 'No-Legs' Charlie got you your first job?"

I nodded. "I thought for sure that I'd be doing repo

work or investigating some piddling insurance claims for local companies."

Rosa leaned forward eagerly. "So what is it, a divorce case? You need a thirty-five-millimeter camera? I can probably get you one from the Media Department at the university."

I shook my head. "Thanks, but no. I have my own camera, and besides, it's just a background check. I'm going to start some surveillance work tonight." I drained my beer and stood up. "I have to get ready for tonight."

Rosa followed me to the door like a puppy. "I wish I could go with you on this stakeout tonight, but I have to work." She had a part-time job at a posh vegetarian restaurant on Newbury Street between Copley Square and Mass Ave, short for Massachusetts Avenue. Bostonians shorten it—don't ask me why, I don't know—just like they shorten Commonwealth Avenue to Comm Ave.

I held up my hand. "Thanks for the thought, but I think I can handle it. You just concentrate on your schoolwork." With that, I left.

My own apartment seemed dismal and depressing after visiting Rosa's sunny and stylish place. I opened the shades to let some light in the living room, but it made the place look more like a battleground at dawn than a livable space.

Sighing, I gathered the things I'd been needing for the surveillance tonight.

While the coffee brewed, I changed into nondescript clothing—gray slacks, a white T-shirt with a gray cardigan over it. I stuffed some warmer clothes into a small backpack for the long March night ahead: gloves, a navy watch cap, and my down vest. Then I made a couple of ham sandwiches.

By the time I finished, it was almost three o'clock and I knew I had to get on the road. If driving to the docks didn't take up most of the time, finding an unobtrusive parking spot where I could keep an eye out for Brian Scanlon might occupy me until the dockworkers started for home.

I gathered my backpack, thermos, camera, and down vest, then brought the whole mess out to the car, threw it in the backseat, and drove off.

# ♣ *Chapter 3*

Boston is very accessible to those who like to walk. I have been known to take the subway (better known to Bostonians as the T) to Government Square, walk to Mass Ave, cross over the Charles River to Cambridge, and continue on to Harvard Square. It's about ten miles all in all, but many times the walk has been preferable to the subway system.

If I have a choice between taking the T and driving a car, I invariably opt for public transportation. But there are some times when driving is required. And in my line of work, an inconspicuous car is a plus.

A 1971 green Datsun 510 is my car of choice. At first I looked at a few Volkswagen Bugs and Chevy Impalas, but my cousin Gino, a car nut, was able to "steer" me in the right direction.

I was given an hour's lecture on the merits of the Datsun 510 compared to the Volkswagen Beetle. The 510 has its own nationwide fan club called the 510 Club. Despite their boxy shape, or maybe because of it, 510s are frequently used in stock car racing.

When Gino and I were strolling around the used car lot, we kept coming back to the little green Datsun 510 and staring at the sticker price.

"Ya know, Angie," Gino began his persuasion tactics, "this 510 will get good mileage, same as a VW Bug, and it'll handle as well, but if you're being followed and you want to shake the tail, the 510'll do it every time."

So I bought the car. And Gino was right. The 510 is a good car to drive during rush hour. It maneuvers between lanes like a dream and zips into spaces most other cars couldn't fit.

The drive to the docks was only across the harbor, but to reach it, I had to drive through the Sumner Tunnel, which is built under the water. The thought of twenty million tons of seawater above me while my car crept along at a snail's pace during rush hour, well, it just gave me the creeps. Fortunately, the tunnel was free at the moment, and I sped through it, relieved to make it to the other side.

Immediately after emerging from the Sumner Tunnel, I turned left to India Wharf. On my way there, I found the Boston Five Cent Savings Bank and deposited Tom Grady's check. I had enough gas, so my only worry was finding a parking space near enough to Brian Scanlon's place of employment on India Wharf. After driving around for almost half an hour, I found a small space just beyond a fire hydrant. Then I settled down for the long wait.

Brian Scanlon worked for the same company as Sheilah. Shamrock Imports did pretty much what the name implied, imported items from Ireland, the stuff no self-respecting Irishman would wear, eat, or decorate his home with: linen tea towels with garish bright green shamrocks, Waterford crystal ashtrays with the words KISS ME, I'M IRISH engraved above a dear little leprechaun face, and cookbooks like *Cooking the Eire Way* that gave directions for making Chocolate Potato Bread. Neon signs that the apocalypse was surely on its way.

I shudder whenever I walk past one of those supposedly quaint little import shops. It's beyond me why other cultures would put up with the incredibly insulting and degrading stereotypical products that pervade these American shops. Maybe it has something to do with the money they make.

Shamrock Imports was just another shipyard warehouse built of crumbling red brick. India Wharf didn't have a fishy smell like Long Wharf. But it also didn't have the best seafood restaurant in the country, the No Name. Every morning when the trawlers came in with their hauls of fish, the No Name got first pick of the fish. My mouth was watering just thinking about it.

I checked the entrance to India Wharf again. There was activity inside the gate, men operating forklifts and cranes, moving large platforms filled with crates from ship to shore, from shore to ship. I caught the faint sound of a whistle and checked my watch. Five o'clock. The men started filing out the gate a few minutes later. I kept a sharp eye out for my man.

There was no reason to conceal myself, I wasn't the only woman sitting in a car, waiting for the breadwinner to climb in so we could head home to a Betty Crocker casserole and a mind-numbing night of television. Still, several men eyed me appreciatively as they passed my car, several calling out such flattering and rhetorical questions as "Hey, chickie. How about it?" and "Yo, mama! I'm yours for the asking!"

I ignored them as best I could—no one came up to the 510 and actually propositioned me directly. I took these to be more of the general "Hi, how ya doin'?" type of remark. I'd gotten some of that in the Marines when I wasn't on duty, so I was used to the attitude.

About fifteen minutes later, Brian Scanlon emerged from the gate, looking much like his picture. He was a tall clean-shaven man with ginger-colored hair, intense blue eyes, and a hawklike nose. With his lean, spare frame, he looked like he was in his mid-thirties. As he passed by my car window, I noticed his big rawboned hands, callused from his work.

Scanlon was accompanied by a short, stocky, brown-haired man in his late forties. They were deep in conversation. I caught a snatch of it before I started my car up, ready to follow my quarry.

"Sheilah isn't feeling well tonight, Mike," Scanlon said as he passed my car. "I don't think we can make it."

Mike replied, "Well, that's too bad, Brian. I was looking forward to introducing you to a friend of mine. I think you have a lot in common."

Scanlon rubbed the back of his neck thoughtfully and said, "Well, I'll try to get out there, but I can't promise anything."

They passed out of range and I wondered where Scanlon and Sheilah Grady were supposed to go tonight. Scanlon and his friend walked about halfway down the block to a large parking lot and disappeared into it. I killed the 510's engine and got out of my car. I walked down to the lot, trying to appear as though I was looking for someone.

I watched Scanlon and his friend stop near an ancient blue Ford station wagon. Scanlon got in the driver's seat and Mike walked on. I got back in my car, started it up, pulled up to the parking lot exit, and waited until the blue station wagon passed me before I slipped smoothly into line behind it.

While the Sumner Tunnel goes from East Boston to Boston proper, the Callahan Tunnel is the reverse. They were built side by side back in the seventies and given different names to keep it straight with Bostonians and to completely confound tourists who want to leave Boston.

Scanlon took the Callahan to East Boston, then turned north onto the aptly named Chelsea Street, which took us directly into the town of Chelsea.

Scanlon and his girlfriend lived in a new fake Colonial-style townhouse on a little street off Central Avenue. He parked his car in a two-door garage. When he didn't come out, I assumed that there was an inner door that led into the house. A moment later, a light went on in the living room and I could see his silhouette against the window shade.

I'd parked my car around the corner and donned my down vest. The weather was still cool, so I didn't look like a complete idiot wearing it. The block was devoid of any cover—no bushes, hedges, or full-grown trees—and I almost despaired of being able to watch the house covertly. That was when I spotted a small cul-de-sac street halfway down the block. It had a perfect view of the townhouse, it was legal to park there, and there was a small fence on that corner that would partially obscure my car, but still afforded me a great view.

I trotted back to my car, drove it to the perfect surveillance site, and settled down. By the time it was dark, I could see two figures in the living room window, a man and a woman. A few hours of watching a stationary object is like watching static on your television set. No, I take that back—static is more exciting because it dances on the screen.

I sat there for the next five and a half hours, finished all my sandwiches, and was working slowly on the coffee. When the thermos was empty, I looked at my watch. It was eleven o'clock and I was about to call it a night when the door to the garage opened and the blue station wagon backed out into the street. Brian Scanlon had decided to meet his friend after all.

This looked interesting—no Sheilah with him, and as I

recalled the conversation at the docks a few hours earlier, his friend Mike had mentioned a friend he wanted Scanlon to meet. Hmmm.

I followed him.

The major roadways were fairly clear for a weeknight and I had no problem following at a distance. It was around the time we reached the Mystic Bridge that I began to regret drinking the coffee. Scanlon took the Mystic Bridge over to Charlestown, then followed the Prison Point Bridge over to Cambridge, which turned into Cambridge Street. From there, Scanlon turned onto Prospect Street.

I noticed we were just southeast of Harvard Square, which meant we were close to Central Square. I began squirming in my seat, and made a solemn vow to refrain from drinking anything the next time I did surveillance.

Sure enough, Scanlon took Harvard Street toward Harvard Square, then turned onto a side street and parked. It was late enough on Monday night for me to find a space a block away from the station wagon. Never mind the fact that there was a fire hydrant there. Any ticket I got would go on Tom Grady's bill. As a former cop, maybe he could get it fixed for me.

When I caught up with him, Scanlon was walking toward Mass Ave, his hands jammed in his pockets, his shoulders hunched over in a furtive manner. I walked with a stiff-legged gait, my breath coming out fast in puffy white clouds, hoping Scanlon would turn in to someplace soon—someplace with a restroom.

Much to my relief, Scanlon entered a bar called the Shandy. It was one of those Irish pubs owned by one of those Irish-Americans who wore buttons that said I'M IRISH AND PROUD OF IT!

I tried to enter casually, as if I were a regular customer rather than a private investigator tailing a suspect. The

Shandy was crowded. Harvard and MIT students were gathered at most of the tables, hunched over their lukewarm half pints of Guinness as if it were a profound experience.

There were several musicians packed in a corner, halfheartedly playing an Irish ballad. The tin whistler wasn't quite in tune with the fiddler and the drummer. It wasn't actually a drum, but a large tambourinelike instrument that the man held, keeping the beat with a stick. They kept stopping at one particular musical phrase and repeating it, trying to get it right. I wondered how long they'd been at it. If they kept it up much longer, it would start to get on my nerves.

The air was stuffy with smoke, sweat, and the hum of voices. I hovered between an empty barstool and the sign to the restrooms, but duty finally won out. With a sigh, I sat down and ordered a Guinness, just to be less conspicuous. A little stout on top of coffee would probably make my bladder scream, but what the hell, I was already uncomfortable. Besides, I'd always wanted to try one. While I waited, I looked around. Brian Scanlon was sitting at a table with Mike. They were leaning toward each other and talking intensely, Scanlon gesturing every once in a while, presumably to make a point.

I wished I could have found a seat closer to them to find out what was being said, but it was probably guy stuff. Besides, I was here to find out anything unusual about Tom Grady's daughter's live-in boyfriend. I assumed my client wanted some sort of information such as Brian Scanlon seeing a babe on the side, selling drugs, or that he was secretly gay. Anything to hang over Scanlon's head, anything that might give Sheilah Grady second thoughts about staying with him.

So far, a night out with the boys wasn't going to cut it. And from what I'd heard outside my car at India Wharf, it sounded as if Sheilah had been planning to come out as well, but she wasn't feeling so hot tonight.

I paid for my Guinness and sipped it slowly while taking in the authentic Irish atmosphere. If I closed my eyes, I could zero in on any conversation at close range. Gee, I might get the mistaken impression that I was in a fake Irish pub on Mass Ave near Harvard Square. Not enough customers talking about working the peat bogs and way too many of them talking about subjects such as mathematics and computers (the MIT students), and business theory (the Harvard contingent) kept me from feeling like I was in a village pub.

I was starting to get bored, thinking of taking that all-important trip to the ladies' room, when another man entered the pub and headed straight over to Scanlon's table. He was a white male in his mid-thirties, of average height and thin almost to the point of emaciation. He had short dark brown, almost black hair and an unpretentious five o'clock shadow. He wore the average Harvard student uniform: jeans, a white T-shirt, and a red wool plaid lumberjack shirt with the sleeves cut off.

If I weren't on an assignment, I might have tried to strike up a conversation with him, invited him home, and fed him lasagna until he got his weight up. There was something very attractive about him. I could almost see the aura of charisma shimmering around him like a halo.

They all stood and Mike appeared to introduce the newcomer to Scanlon. All three men looked furtively around and when their eyes rested on me, I pretended to study the decor above and to the right of their heads; it was a giant shamrock with the words, THE WEARIN' OF THE GREEN written on it in gold glitter.

When I chanced to look back at their table, they had left, heading toward a door in the back of the room. I hopped off my barstool and walked over to the bartender, who was busy mixing an imported beer with something else.

"Excuse me," I said, leaning toward him. I fluttered my eyelashes for effect and he smiled. "That man looks very familiar to me." I pointed to the thin, dark-haired man with Mike and Brian. "But I can't recall his name and it would be embarrassing to go up to him without remembering. You wouldn't happen to know him, would you?"

The bartender, a large, soft man with almost girlish features, nodded. "Oh, yes. He's been coming in here for several weeks, almost every night. His name is Seamus McRaney. I've overheard him talking to some others around here. He works for an organization called the International League for the Advancement of Peace."

I slipped him a five and thanked him. The three men had disappeared through the back door and I would have followed them, but suddenly there was an immovable object blocking the entrance. He stood well over six feet. As I peered up at his face, he looked a little like Dan Blocker to me.

"Excuse me," I said for the second time that night. "I need to get in there."

He crossed his arms and said in a rather high voice, "Sorry, lady. This room's being used. It's off limits."

*Where had this guy come from anyway?* I thought. I hoped he was the stereotypical jock and wouldn't notice that I was lying to him.

"I thought this was the way to the ladies' room." I hated myself for looking up at him in a flirtatious manner. But I didn't think I'd win this human monolith over by telling him the truth—that I was following one of the fellows who disappeared into that back room.

He must have bought my lie because he gripped one of my elbows steadily and steered me toward a small hallway to the left. With his other hand, he pointed to the RESTROOMS sign.

"It's that way, lady. This other room is a meeting room." He smiled, revealing a missing tooth. Great. Just when Brian Scanlon was starting to interest me, I got stopped by a cross between Arnold Schwarzenegger and Alfred E. Neuman.

I waved my thanks to him and staggered gratefully down the hall to the ladies' room. After a few minutes, I slipped back into the pub and took a look around. The behemoth was nowhere in sight, but that didn't mean he hadn't slipped into the meeting room. I wasn't prepared to meet him again at cross purposes without a loaded elephant gun on hand.

Scanlon and his pals weren't around, either. I had two choices: either stick around and drink pints of stout until they appeared again, or leave. Even if they did emerge from that room, I probably wouldn't learn anything I didn't already know. I'd just end up following Scanlon back to Chelsea, then give up for the night.

But I stayed because of my sense of duty. A good private investigator should always stick with his subject until he feels there's nothing more to be gained from the surveillance. And then he or she should stay around an hour longer, just to be sure.

Less than an hour and five passes later, the three men appeared again. I watched them from the bar mirror until they left the joint. The Shandy was preparing to close, so I joined the exodus.

Outside, it was clear that Seamus McRaney, Mike, and Brian Scanlon were going their separate ways. Although I was interested in McRaney, I kept Brian Scanlon in my sight. I could get more information on Seamus McRaney and the ILAP organization tomorrow.

I followed Scanlon back to Chelsea and waited in my

car for another long, cold hour. Scanlon's house remained dark. When I was past sure he was in for the night, I drove home and crawled into bed myself.

Lying in the darkness, I turned over the surveillance done tonight. So far, Brian Scanlon hadn't done anything illegal or immoral that I could report to Tom Grady—but my curiosity was piqued. Slipping into an off-limits back room for a secret meeting certainly seemed suspicious to me.

## ♣ Chapter 4

$\mathcal{I}$ could hear the phone ringing as I walked down the hall to my office. I was carrying a take-out bag in one arm and balancing a cup of coffee on top of a small box in my other. The box contained books which I planned to use to fill shelf space. Last night on my way home, I'd passed an import store. On impulse, I ducked in and came across a sale on bookcases.

After reading the *Boston Globe*'s second-page coverage of yesterday's Haymarket corpse (he'd been a freelance journalist), I'd spent most of this morning putting together the bookcase I'd bought while waiting for a call back from my friend Raina, who works in the East Boston precinct. The impatiently ringing phone was probably her calling me back with the information I'd requested.

I sprinted down the hall as best I could, getting my key ready to jam into the lock. I'd learned more than discipline in the Marines. Ten seconds and three rings later, I was inside my office. As quickly and carefully as possible, I put down the things I was carrying, body-surfed across the desk, and grabbed the receiver. "Hello?" I shouted. Dignity took over and I stuttered, "I—I mean, Angela Matelli here. How may I help you?"

God, I sounded like a prissy receptionist. I'd have to work on my delivery when answering the phone.

A loud laugh on the other end almost pierced my eardrum. I instinctively held the phone away. "God, Angie, you sound so confused." It was Sophia, she of the two brats and string of biker boyfriends. What a class act.

I sighed, exasperated. "What do you want, Soph?"

"I hate it when you call me that, Ang. Just wondered how you were doing," she said, sounding hurt. I didn't waste time feeling guilty. Sophia was a good little actress when she wanted to be.

We were only a year apart in age. The antagonistic relationship between us was one of the reasons no one noticed the friction between Ma and Rosa until after Sophia got married and I joined the Marines.

"I'm doing fine," I replied, staring down at my coffee cup. It had toppled over, but fortunately it had a plastic lid on it and was only leaking a small amount of hot liquid onto my book box. I quickly righted it. "What do you want, Soph?"

There was a small silence. She was probably wondering if it was worth the effort to remind me again not to use the shortened version of her name. She must have decided it wasn't because she asked, "Has Ma talked to you yet?"

"I talked to her yesterday morning, but not today."

An impatient sigh on the other end of the line made me suspect that Ma had, again, been delegated to pave the way to a more amicable relationship between us sisters so Sophia could drop one of her bombshells on me. She never called me unless she wanted something.

It had always been that way with us. Sophia was the biggest manipulator of all time. Unfortunately, I was the only one in the family who ever recognized her little games for what they were. I learned early on not to place too much importance on the idea of sisterly love when it came to Sophia and her requests. I knew that everything Sophia asked for, she got. And if she didn't get it, she'd stamp her pretty little feet and pout appealingly until the giver gave in.

I was getting irritable just thinking about it, so I asked brusquely, "Well, what did you call for, Sophia? Money?"

"No," came the reluctant reply.

"That's usually what you've called for in the past," I said dryly. "Well? Out with it. I can't stay on the line all day. I'm expecting an important phone call."

"I need a place to live. I'm being evicted from my apartment."

I hoped that Sophia would mistake my silence for a dead line.

"Angie? Come on, this isn't funny."

"Do you hear me laughing?" I asked. "So you're being kicked out of your apartment—what does this have to do with me?" As if I didn't know.

"Well, you have that whole first floor open. No tenant. I thought I could move in."

This is where I started laughing. Hysterically. Scenes of Sophia and me living in the same city, let alone the same building, were, well, laughable.

Sophia took on a stern tone. "Angela Matelli, you stop right this minute and listen to me."

I got my laughter under control and replied, "Right. I'm here. What did you get thrown out for?"

"What makes you think I'm being thrown out?" my sister asked indignantly.

"Oh, I don't know," I replied innocently. "It couldn't have anything to do with your thug boyfriends, your late work and social hours, or those two darling monsters you're raising. Or rather, Ma is raising."

"Don't talk to me like that." Sophia raised her voice. "My boyfriends are nice to me, and you know perfectly well that my work as a cocktail waitress requires me to stay until the bar closes."

Nothing had been said in defense of Michael and Stephanie. There were some problems that even Sophia couldn't ignore.

"You might try paying your rent on time, then," I suggested.

"Look, sis." *Sis?* This had to be serious. "I don't have the time to go looking for another apartment. And you know what the rents around Boston are like. Couldn't you help your own sister out?"

"I did," I reminded her shortly. "And Rosa is doing just fine. She's studying hard and pays her rent on the first of the month."

"Aw, come on," Sophia entreated me. In a low voice, she said, "Angie, don't make me beg you."

I couldn't let her dangle too much longer. I could already hear Ma's voice grating across the phone lines. The last thing I wanted was to get in an argument with Ma. She always won, one way or another. If not with reason, then with the universal motherly weapon—guilt.

"Okay." I sighed reluctantly. "But you know that the first-floor apartment is smaller than mine or Rosa's—it only has one bedroom. You'd need to fix it up a bit. A little paint wouldn't hurt."

"Maybe Rosa would trade with me—"

"Maybe I won't rent that apartment to you," I said, hoping there was enough of a threat in my tone so Sophia would take me seriously. I reached for my coffee cup and pulled the lid off carefully. "Besides, it does have a walk-in closet that can be converted into a bedroom—maybe for Michael."

She backed off. "Okay, okay. It was just a suggestion."

"I'm serious, Sophia." I knew how my older sister could be when she got an idea in her head. "Rosa has worked damned hard on her apartment and I won't let you bully her into moving," I warned, adding, "Your arrangement with me is temporary. And any painting or fixing up will be done by you because your rent will be very low. Is that understood?" I took a sip of coffee and promptly sloshed some on my good jeans.

"Understood," she replied in an airy tone. "And thanks, Angie."

"No problem," I said, trying not to sound too irritated. "Now I have to clear this line. I'm expecting a call."

I hung up with misgivings. To say that I wasn't happy with this turn of events was the understatement of the year. But I couldn't turn my back on my own flesh and blood. Michael and Stephanie had to have a roof over their heads. Sophia, well, I wasn't as concerned about her. She always managed to land on her feet.

I went down the hall to the ladies' restroom and dabbed some cold water on the spot. At least the coffee hadn't spilled on my new red blouse. Returning to my office, I turned to the task of opening my rapidly cooling braciola sub, stuffed steak rolls in marinara sauce on a roll. It was so good to eat familiar meals again, the food I grew up with. In the service, the closest I got to Italian food was on Thursday nights when the mess hall would invariably have some loathsome cold, clammy noodles in barely warm tomato sauce. They called it "Spaghetti Night."

Two bites into my now-cold sub, the phone rang. I jumped and some of the tomato sauce from the braciola dribbled onto my blouse. I groaned and closed my eyes in disgust. Another trip to the ladies' room down the hall. The phone rang a second time and I picked it up.

"Angela Matelli, private investigations," I said around a mouthful of food.

I recognized the giggle on the other end of the line.

"Honestly, Angie. I was going to ask you what you were doing for lunch, but it sounds like you've already taken care of it."

"Hi, Raina. Actually, I wouldn't mind meeting you for a cup of coffee." I looked ruefully at my braciola and the lukewarm cup of take-out coffee still sitting on top of my book box.

"I have the information you asked for. It wasn't hard to find something on Brian Scanlon, but Seamus McRaney, now, he's another story. Kind of an enigma, you know?"

"Yeah, I know," I replied. "Well, any rumors or stories you've heard will help."

We agreed to meet at a little coffee shop in East Boston in half an hour. Which meant I had to hustle out of my office and leave my sandwich to congeal. Maybe the mice would enjoy it. After getting as much of the stain out of my blouse as possible, and consoling myself with the fact that it was tomato sauce on red material, I grabbed my jacket and left for the T station. It had warmed up a bit since I'd gotten to work this morning, but it still wasn't shirtsleeves weather. The subway was running like a well-oiled machine today. It took me only fifteen minutes to get to East Boston.

Raina was waiting for me at a table. She had on a pretty green print dress which was more appropriate for spring weather, but then again, we all hope for warmer weather in our own way. For as long as I'd known her, Raina had dressed according to her own whims and not according to the weather. I did notice that she had a black wool winter coat slung carelessly over the back of her chair. A plain manila folder sat on the table in front of her.

She was pretty in a WASPish way. Short and fair-haired, Raina James was in her late twenties. Actually, she was my age. It was sometimes hard for me to believe that my childhood friend had been married twice, both times to SOBs. She always went for the type who wore torn T-shirts and yelled, "Stel-la!"

As the dispatcher for the East Boston precinct, Raina had access to just about every department in the area and could pull up information easily. As long as her boss wasn't around. He probably wouldn't be too thrilled to find out that his dispatcher was spending part of the tax-payers' dollars doing little favors for me.

Of course, he hadn't grown up with me like Raina had. We got into quite a few scrapes back in the old days, but we survived them all and kept in touch.

The coffee shop was decorated in fifties style, but it didn't look as if any thought had gone into it. My feeling was that the owner had just been too lazy to update the place. But they served a decent cup of Italian roast here, and from what Raina had said on the phone about Scanlon, I would probably need to toss back a few.

"I already ordered," she apologized.

As if on cue, the waitress came over with Raina's order, a large chef's salad with Italian dressing on the side. I ordered coffee and a bagel with cream cheese.

Raina stared at me. "I thought you ate already."

"Yeah,"—I shrugged—"I started to, but never finished."

She looked contrite. I waved a hand and said, "It's not your fault. Sophia called. It's a long story. Remind me to tell you about it sometime."

My friend's face brightened with understanding. She knew Sophia well.

We turned to business.

"This was everything I could dig up on Brian Scanlon," Raina said as she took out ten pages stapled together. I started to look through them and did a double-take. Raina noticed my reaction and asked, "What's wrong?"

I shook my head. "Oh, nothing. I didn't expect him to be in his early forties. He looks younger in person."

"Must be the nurturing prison environment," Raina replied dryly.

I read down the rap sheet: arson at age thirteen, car theft at fourteen, member of a radical political organization at sixteen, responsible for violence at antiwar demonstrations at college when he was eighteen, and terrorist bombings at twenty-one. Brian had been a busy boy. Until he was arrested for planting a bomb in a Dorchester police station. It was at the height of the Vietnam War, when college campus antiwar activities had practically become a cottage industry.

Unfortunately, the young Scanlon fell in with the wrong crowd, an anarchic group that was not only antiwar, but antilife. At the time that Brian Scanlon was caught, there had been a rash of bombings in several New England states and law enforcement was pushing to get hard time for any terrorist caught. He was sent away back in 1969 for the maximum conviction in Massachusetts—eighteen years. Scanlon was paroled after fifteen years. Surprisingly, he'd kept his nose clean on the outside for the last six years.

Reading on, I learned that Brian Scanlon had been given a full scholarship to MIT. *A good place to learn how to make bombs,* I thought.

There were several more pages with information about Scanlon's push for prisoner's rights in Walpole Penitentiary, and the unsubstantiated comments about Scanlon's participation in prison fights, attempts to escape, and more violent demonstrations in which prison guards were taken hostage several times during Scanlon's stay. The fact that no one would ever come forward as a witness to Scanlon's activities in Walpole said something about the man's ability to generate loyalty. There were reports that Scanlon was a thinker and a leader, not a doer. And only those who do, get caught.

For such an intelligent man, I couldn't understand how he could end up on the wrong side of the law. He could have become a lawyer or a doctor. He could have found a cure for cancer or ended world hunger. And why was he hooking up with the International League for the Advancement of Peace?

I looked up at Raina, who was chasing a piece of lettuce around her bowl with her fork. "This is pretty incredible stuff," I said, shaking my head. "This guy is very bright, but not exactly the type you want to bring home to meet Daddy." The waitress tossed my bagel on the table in front of me. I started in on it.

"Unless Daddy is a terrorist," Raina quipped. She finally speared the morsel of rabbit food and, chewing, said, "Now you're probably wondering about Seamus McRaney."

I paged through to the end, not finding any data on him. "Yeah. What gives?"

She finished chewing and replied, "Well, there wasn't anything on the computer files—well, nothing that I could get into. There was a security lock and I couldn't get past calling up his name. But I have a friend at the *Boston Globe* in the news department. He knows most of what's going on with international terrorism—he's made it his specialty. I couldn't get him on the phone. He was out covering a fire or something like that. You might want to go down and see him."

"What's his name?" I asked.

"Craig Cohen. I got his secretary on the phone and made an appointment for you this afternoon."

I drew myself up indignantly and said, "That's very good of you, Raina, but you should have asked me first. I might have already been booked with engagements this afternoon."

She grinned. "And are you?"

I slumped over and shook my head, a smile on my face. "No."

I magnanimously paid the lunch check and, after thanking Raina for her help, we parted ways. My appointment with the *Globe* reporter was for two o'clock. That gave me enough time to jog down to the Maverick Square station. I hopped the T and, transferring to the green line at Government Center, then transferring one stop later to the red line, rode out to the *Boston Globe* offices in Dorchester.

I arrived with fifteen minutes to spare, which was good because the *Boston Globe* offices were a confusing maze. The receptionist in the lobby had me sign in and gave me a temporary pass, then gave me complicated directions to Craig Cohen's desk. The newsroom was one big mass of cubicles filled with desks and computers and the busy sound of reporters tap-tap-tapping away at their keyboards in order to make the next deadline.

After several wrong turns and getting more directions from other people along the way, I arrived at a uniform cubicle where, glasses askew, a harried-looking middle-aged man was sorting through a stack of computer paper. I didn't think anyone wore horn-rimmed glasses anymore, but apparently no one ever told this guy they were out of date. He wore jeans and a long-sleeved light blue shirt under one of those red sleeveless V-neck sweaters, the kind that had been popular in the sixties. Apparently he was under the impression that the sweaters were still in fashion. The sign on the outside of the cubicle told me that this was Craig Cohen.

I stood just inside his office and, after being ignored for a full minute, I cleared my throat.

"Uh, Mr. Cohen?"

He stopped sorting paper and turned around. His glasses were perched on his nose and his thinning hair was mussed, as if he'd spent a lot of time running his hands through it.

"What do you want?" he demanded sharply.

"We have an appointment," I reminded him, quickly adding, "Raina James sent me here. I can see you're busy, so I won't take up much of your time."

He seemed to think about it for a moment, then nodded. "Okay, as long as you don't mind if I work while we're talking. The *Globe* has to be put to bed soon and I'm still trying to find the last paragraph to my article. I seem to have lost my notes." He looked around distractedly at his desk and his tiny office space.

I spotted some lined yellow sheets with scribbles on them, lying crumpled under his desk near his chair. Pointing to them, I asked, "Could those be what you're looking for?"

Cohen twisted around, grabbed them, and gave them a cursory glance. A pleased look crossed his face. With a relieved sigh, he replied, "Thank you, Miss . . . ?"

"Angela Matelli, private investigator," I said as we shook hands. He had a warm, dry grip. Very pleasant.

He chuckled. "Private eye, huh? I might have known. I could use you around the office more often. What can I do for you, Miss Matelli?"

"Tell me everything you know about the ILAP and Seamus McRaney."

Cohen's face took on a more businesslike look. "Ah,

yes. Mr. McRaney. He's back in town, right?"

"As far as I know. I was following someone the other night," I explained, "and my man met Seamus McRaney at the Shandy."

Cohen was leaning back in his chair, his arms crossed, rubbing his chin thoughtfully. "Well, I'll tell you the scuttlebutt, Miss Matelli. But what I tell you has never been confirmed. McRaney's too smart for that."

He turned to his notes, consulting them over the tops of his glasses. "The International League for the Advancement of Peace was formed about ten years ago in Belfast," Cohen began. "Seamus McRaney is the son of an IRA member who was killed in an ambush by the British army. Publicly, McRaney has denounced his deceased father's activities and vowed to help end the conflict in his country through peaceful means. That's where ILAP comes in."

I asked, "What does ILAP do specifically?"

He nodded and replied, "Well, they profess to help all those who have been sent to prison for political reasons. So far, the only people I see McRaney's organization helping are captured terrorists like members of the IRA or alleged members of the IRA."

He leaned back in his chair, putting his hands behind his head, and continued, "And although we can't substantiate it, it seems that after every time ILAP comes over to the States to raise money for their cause, more violence breaks out back in Belfast. We suspect that they use American money to buy guns and secretly transport them back home. Of course, no one has been able to prove it, but just read the international news after ILAP has packed up and gone back to Northern Ireland. I can guarantee that there will be a rise in bloodshed."

I nodded and said, "Then it's possible that my suspect is somehow involved in all of this. He does have a history of political dissidence. He's an ex-con."

Cohen frowned. "What's his name?"

I told him and briefly laid out Brian Scanlon's history.

"I seem to recall his name from my research into political activism back in the sixties. I think he was a minor character who went to prison for a bomb scare. I don't know what his connection to McRaney is, but I'd have to be a cynic and suggest that he's probably up to no good."

I thanked him for his time and started to leave. He called me back. "Miss Matelli, if by chance you uncover some interesting information and need some help, I'm available. But I expect to have first chance on the story." He handed me a business card with his office and home numbers on it. "Call me day or night."

I returned the courtesy by giving him my home and work numbers, grinned, and replied, "You drive a hard bargain, but I think I can keep my end of the deal."

♣ *Chapter 5*

*I*t was three-thirty, almost rush hour, and there was no reason for me to go back to the office, so I took the T back to East Boston. Rosa's apartment was dark and silent, so I assumed she was at work or school, which was not that much of an assumption, since she went to school in the daytime and worked five nights a week, including weekends.

I wasn't looking forward to talking to Tom Grady, but I couldn't put it off much longer. When I got up to my apartment, I called him.

"Ah, Miss Matelli," he said when he answered the phone. "I have company right now. My daughter's over here."

I can take a hint. "Can you meet me at ten tomorrow morning at my office?" I asked. "I can give you a report on what I've discovered so far and you can decide whether you want me to pursue this inquiry or end it."

"That would be fine," he replied. "See you tomorrow."

After hanging up the phone, I looked in my pathetically stocked cupboard and took inventory: pasta shells, a can of kidney beans, garlic, olive oil, tomato paste. My refrigerator held one lone onion and some ground beef that was starting to smell a little gamy. All the ingredients for a hearty Italian soup called pasta fagioli. While I was fixing it, I was wishing there were a couple of good Chinese take-out places nearby. The problem with living in East Boston was that I felt as if I were isolated from the rest of Boston's melting pot.

I was out of bread, so while the fagioli simmered, I ran down to the corner store and picked up a loaf of bread, along with a bottle of good red table wine, green peppers, a dozen eggs, marinated artichoke hearts, prosciutto, parmesan and provolone cheese, and a bag of homemade fettucine noodles. It would last me about a week, considering how often I ate out.

Back at home, I settled down with a bowl of the soup, a hunk of bread and cheese, and a glass of wine. I wished I had someone to come home to, even a pet. I made a mental note to look into getting a puppy or kitten. I wasn't particular, but a kitten might be more practical. A cat could fend for itself, whereas a dog seemed to be totally dependent on its owner. Besides, I disliked a bootlicker. I'd gotten enough of that in the service.

There wasn't much on the tube except for the news. Halfway through the evening, I dropped a compact disc in my player and, listening to Patsy Cline's soothing voice, stared at my barren apartment as I tried to decide what colors to paint the walls and what kind of furniture I'd be most comfortable with. Maybe I'd stop in and look around that import store where I got the bookcase, when I had a little time later this week.

As I worked my way through my third glass of wine, I heard the entryway door slam and footsteps clump up the stairs. They stopped on the second floor and the jangle of keys told me that Rosa was home from work. I debated whether to go down there and talk to her, but I looked at my watch. It was one-thirty in the morning. Too late to be calling, even if she was my sister. In fact, it was time for me to call it a night, so I finished my wine, turned off the music, and did just that.

The phone woke me up. My bedside clock told me it was eight-thirty. I'd forgotten to set the alarm and had overslept. I had to be in the office by ten to meet with Tom Grady.

I jumped out of bed and, in a gravelly voice, answered, "Hello?"

*Nothing quite as delightful as morning breath,* I thought, grimacing.

"Angie? This is your mother speaking."

"Ma, I just woke up," I complained, my voice a gravelly rumble. "Can this wait?"

"I just wanted you to know how pleased I am that all you girls will soon be living together," she trilled. "That was very thoughtful of you, dear."

I cleared my throat and replied, "Yeah, it was thoughtful of me." I tried to keep the sarcasm out of my tone. "Look, Ma, I have to be at the office at ten. I really have to hang up now."

"All right, dear. Just one more little detail."

I sighed. "I'm listening."

"When can Sophia and her brood move in?"

I scratched my itchy scalp, desperately wanting a shower. "Let's see. It's ready to move in right now. She just needs to pick up the keys."

"Well, dear, I talked to her last night and she said you'd be fixing the place up for her this weekend. Don't you want to paint it to make it nice for your sister?"

I was silent for a moment. Sophia had been feeding Ma false information. What a surprise. She didn't want to do any work on the place herself. I thought we'd had a clear understanding when I talked to her on the phone yesterday.

With as much control as I could muster, I said, "Ma, she's getting the place practically for free. What does she want, a marble fireplace and a crystal chandelier as well?"

Ma sounded hurt. "Angie, I just thought you'd want—"

I interrupted her, tired of being manipulated by Sophia. "I want to take a shower and get down to the office at ten to meet my client. If Sophia doesn't like the deal, she can go apartment hunting instead. My offer was for a temporary place to stay. In exchange for a drastic reduction in rent, Sophia has agreed to fix the place up to her liking while she's looking for a more spacious apartment for herself, her kids, and whatever sleazy boyfriend she's seeing at the moment. Have I made it clear enough?"

"This is your mother you're talking to, Angela Agnes Matelli! I don't see what's so terrible about fixing up that apartment for your own flesh and blood."

She used Agnes on me. I winced. I hated my middle name and Ma knew it. Whenever she was angry with me, she wielded that middle name like a loaded .357 Magnum.

I replied, "You always take Sophia's side, don't you? You just can't see that she's a manipulating little bitch. She's even got us yelling at each other over something that should be just between her and me. Stop fighting her battles for her, Ma. And for once, why don't you look at the situation from the other side?"

"Ever since you got out of the Marines, Angela," Ma said, taking that dangerously low tone with me, "you've been getting help from your family." She was on a roll now. "I didn't see you turn any favors down. Now it's your turn to do something for family and you act like it's a burden. And don't call your sister a bitch again. She's had a hard life."

"Oh, and whose fault is that?" I asked in a nasty tone, adding, "I don't pick her men for her, and neither do you. And I am doing a favor for Sophia. She and her kids would be out in the street if I didn't have that apartment free. But our understanding is that this was a temporary arrangement." I continued firmly, "And I won't have her using you to get at me. If she wants to decorate the apartment, she has carte blanche. She has two arms and two legs, she has a steady job, and she has a hell of a lot better taste than me when it comes to decorating. If she wants the apartment painted and furnished, she's going to have to supply the time and energy to do it. The subject is closed. I have a meeting in an hour and I have to hang up now."

I waited. Ma usually liked the last word. Our family fights were the quintessential Italian type—big blowups, lots of yelling and threatening each other, and five minutes later, it's as if we'd never had the fight.

Ma changed the topic of conversation, as close to admitting I'm in the right as she's ever come. "Will I see you on Sunday night for dinner as usual? Your brothers will be there with their families. Remind Rosa, too."

I felt drained from the argument, but I managed to tell her that I'd be there. Then I hung up, put the coffee on, and jumped in the shower. I checked the temperature outside the bathroom window and discovered that it was warm for early March. When I was out of the shower, I dressed in gray flannel slacks, black cotton blouse, to fit my mood, and an oversize maroon cotton knit sweater. I brushed my hair and put on some earrings so I felt a little more feminine. Then I poured a cup of strong black coffee and gulped it down before rushing out to catch the T.

I got to the office with five minutes to spare, and spent that time doodling on one of my yellow legal pads. Brian Scanlon's case file was perched on a corner of my desk.

Tom Grady knocked on my door ten minutes after ten o'clock. In Boston, that's a pretty good record. If he'd taken the T, the trains were probably running on time, and if he'd driven, it was a miracle that he'd found a parking spot in the North End.

I invited him in.

"Miss Matelli, I hope I'm not too late," Grady said, shutting the office door and sitting down in the chair reserved for clients.

"Not at all. I was just going over your case." I grabbed the file, opened it, and shuffled the papers nervously before beginning. How do you tell a client that his hunch was not only right, but paid off in spades?

Grady narrowed his eyes knowingly and said, "You found something, didn't you?"

I met his eyes and nodded shortly. "I certainly have, Mr. Grady. Your feelings were right." I recited the events of my night of surveillance, up until he met Seamus McRaney. There, I paused and watched my client's face, trying to gauge his reaction. Instead of a shocked or worried look, his expression was impassive.

I decided to test his knowledge of the Irish Republican Army because I was beginning to get a hunch of my own. "You do know who Seamus McRaney is, don't you?" I asked.

Tom Grady smiled slightly and, in a tone implying that he already knew, asked, "Why don't you tell me, Miss Matelli? That's what I'm paying you for."

I hesitated, then launched into an explanation about Seamus McRaney and his organization, ILAP. All the time, Grady listened, nodding encouragement silently when I paused. I got the feeling that my client was surprised to hear the rumors about ILAP being a front for gunrunning.

Finally I came to Brian Scanlon's background.

"Brian Scanlon is an ex-con, Mr. Grady. I don't know if your daughter knows, but you might want to sit her down and have a talk with her." I rattled off Scanlon's record, then told Tom Grady that Scanlon served fifteen years of an eighteen-year sentence in Walpole for planting a bomb in a Dorchester police station. I added, "I'm not sure how this ties in with Scanlon consorting with Seamus McRaney, but my feeling is that their association might not be innocent."

Tom Grady sighed deeply and passed a large hand over his face. "It certainly doesn't sound good. I was hoping that I was wrong."

"If you like," I ventured, "I could look into this more thoroughly for you. You still have two more days of my services available. It may look bad on the surface, but perhaps the rumors about ILAP aren't true. Maybe Scanlon and McRaney are just friends—"

Grady shot a rueful smile in my direction and finished, "And maybe they only went into the Shandy's guarded back room to shoot some pool?" He shook his head and said, "No, thank you for your offer, Miss Matelli. But I'm not interested in bringing Scanlon and McRaney to justice, only in learning the truth. Keep the rest of what I paid you as a bonus." He stood up. "Besides, you must have more to do than worry about my case."

*Yeah, a calendar loaded with lunch dates,* I thought. Out loud I said, "Good luck, Mr. Grady. Give me a call if I can be of any other service to you. If you have a talk with your daughter and need my corroboration to make her understand how serious this is, I'll be happy to give it, free of charge."

We shook hands, he thanked me again, then he left.

I sat back in my chair, glad of the silence and the chance to let the tension drain out of me after what had just happened in my office. It was obvious that Tom Grady had already known a good deal of what I told him. But I must have provided the confirmation that he needed, and the tangible proof that a relationship, however tenuous, existed between Brian Scanlon, the ex-con, and Seamus McRaney, a possible IRA terrorist. But what was the connection?

Now that Tom Grady had the information, what did he intend to do with it? I could think of two possibilities: tell Sheilah and let her make up her own mind, or blackmail Scanlon with the information to get him out of Grady's daughter's life.

I didn't like either possibility, but then, I wasn't a retired cop whose only daughter was living with an ex-con who once tried to blow up a police station.

## ♣ Chapter 6

$\mathcal{I}$ had arranged to take on investigating some insurance claims for a local insurance agency, Leone and Associates. Actually, the work was arranged for me by my Aunt Louisa. She knew the parents of the owner of the company. As it turned out, I knew Robert Leone, who owned the joint; he'd been a member of my graduating class. In fact, he'd been my high school sweetheart.

It was quite a surprise for both of us when I walked through the door early Wednesday afternoon. Bob was surprised that the girl he'd dumped in high school was an ex-Marine and currently a private investigator, and I was surprised that the captain of our basketball team was now fifty pounds overweight and prematurely balding.

Bob grinned sheepishly as his hand glided over the patch of smooth pate. "It's those darn kids who're making me lose my hair," he said. "There's three of them and Teresa and I have a fourth one on the way."

"Not Teresa Marchetti," I replied, trying not to sound too aghast. Teresa had been one of the golden girls in our alma mater: head cheerleader, class secretary, editor of our yearbook, homecoming queen—need I go on?

Bob blushed, or rather flushed, and nodded. "Yep. We

got married right out of high school and had our first one almost immediately."

I stifled the urge to crow, *So it was true!* Just before we'd graduated, there'd been a rumor that Teresa was pregnant.

I needed the job, so instead I smiled like an idiot and bobbed my head, avoiding his eyes for a moment by looking around his dumpy little office. It was dark and the decor was in shades of brown: the carpet, the curtains, the desk, the lamps, the chairs, and the couch. Even the phone was brown. I had only been sitting there for five minutes before I started to get the feeling that I wanted to slit my wrists. I seemed to recall that Teresa Marchetti wore a lot of brown in our senior year. I wondered if she'd done the decorating.

Suddenly I wanted to be anyplace else but Leone and Associates. I couldn't see how Bob Leone stood it, but the cramped and dingy atmosphere didn't seem to bother him. It was probably his home away from home.

Bob leered at me and asked, "How come you and I broke up, Angie? I always liked you."

I blurted it out before I had a chance to think clearly. "Because I wouldn't put out for you, Bob."

Fortunately, he thought I was kidding. Besides, he needed an investigator, so I was hired on a contract basis.

Although the work was mind-numbing routine questioning of witnesses, it wasn't a totally uneventful few days for me. For instance, on my way home from the office on Friday night, I was mugged. Until it happened to me, I never thought much about what it felt like to be a mugging victim.

I'd been working in my office until ten o'clock. Just before I left, I tugged open the bottom left-hand drawer. I drew out my Star to carry with me as I walked to the T in the dark. Just in case. Since I was anxious to leave, I stuck the gun in my bag instead of in my waistband.

During the day, it had rained steadily. There was a light drizzle as I walked down to the State Street subway station. I turned down Salt Street, a short cut to Merchants Row. It seemed like a good idea at the time because Merchants Row would take me through the more populated areas of Faneuil Hall. But Salt Street is a narrow little street, almost a glorified alleyway, with a streetlamp at both ends and no light in between. I walked cautiously down the middle, unaware that there was anyone behind me until an arm caught me across my throat and a knifepoint jabbed viciously at the small of my back.

"Be quiet, lady, and maybe I won't hurt you," a raspy voice ordered. "Give me your wallet." There was an odd inflection to my attacker's voice, but I wasn't in any position to try and place it.

My whole body stiffened—even my brain froze. Then the Marine in me took over and I went into automatic. *Give the guy what he wants and he'll go away,* I thought. Only in my heart, I didn't believe it. I tugged at my shoulder bag, but the strap caught on one of those decorative buttons on the shoulder of my jacket. I remembered the gun and hoped that my assailant wouldn't feel its bulk through the purse's fabric.

"I'm afraid you're going to have to let up on my shoulder for a second," I apologized in a shaky voice. "I can't get the strap free."

The mugger did just that, which gave me the room to twist around and push his knife-in-hand away from me. Then I threw a right kick to his knee and did a spin kick to his hand. I heard the knife clatter to the pavement. My assailant was bent over, groaning.

I moved toward him to see if he was all right—something we are told *not* to do in self-defense class—and he straightened up, clipping me in the jaw with his right fist, then smashing his left into my nose. I staggered back, stunned from the blows.

When I regained my balance, the mugger had grabbed his knife and was moving toward me again. I stuck my hand into my bag and pulled out my gun, assuming a stance while training my weapon on him. The only phrase that came to mind is one that bad actors use on TV cop shows.

"Freeze!" I yelled.

My attacker hesitated, then turned and half ran, half limped toward Merchants Row. I considered shooting at him, but immediately dismissed it. The shots might go wild and injure an innocent bystander at the end of the alleyway, or shooting at him might antagonize the mugger enough that he would take someone else hostage. Besides, I could be arrested for impersonating a police officer. Yeah, that gun came in real handy.

I followed him, jogging at an easy pace until I reached the well-lit area of Faneuil Hall, a tourist's haven. Looking around for any sign of my assailant, I realized I'd lost the son of a bitch. Maybe I should have tried harder. Too bad. I was in the mood for a fight and would have loved to trade blows with the bastard.

But the moment was lost. It was nearly ten-thirty, and the Friday night bar-hoppers were milling around, leaving restaurants and bars in the area. Passersby threw strange looks my way. I must have looked a sight with my disheveled clothes, bloody nose, and a gun in my hand. After hastily shoving the Star back into my purse, I explored the damage done to my face. Touching my jaw gingerly made me flinch; I was certain that I would have a prominent bruise there by tomorrow morning. But when I touched my nose, it didn't seem to be broken.

When I contemplated visiting a nearby police station

to fill out a report, I realized that I hadn't lost any money and hadn't gotten a good look at the mugger. All I knew was that he was a white male, approximately five feet ten inches tall. There had to be half a million five-foot-ten white guys walking around Boston. Some help I would have been. So I scrapped the idea.

Looking back on the whole incident, I found it odd that he hadn't just grabbed my purse back there on Salt Street. But I shrugged it off, chalking it up to a nervous and inexperienced mugger.

Before continuing on my merry way, I ducked into a lounge near Faneuil Hall and used their ladies' room to freshen myself up. I was right about my face. I looked like I'd lost a prizefight. The nose was slightly swollen and would probably be bruised, but his punch must have glanced off instead of breaking it. I was relieved because I was rather fond of the shape of my nose.

After washing my face and combing out my hair, I walked up to the bar, climbed onto a stool, and ordered a bourbon straight up.

While the bartender poured my drink, he gave me a look that told me I didn't belong there. I took in my surroundings for the first time. It was an upscale place, ladies wearing designer cocktail dresses and gentlemen wearing gold Rolexes and power ties. My jeans and white T-shirt would have looked more appropriate in a place frequented by construction workers instead of yuppies. My bourbon came to five dollars. Since I wasn't in a good mood, just to irritate everyone, I nursed my one drink for half an hour before leaving.

By the time I got back to East Boston, it was nearly midnight. I entered my apartment building and dragged my carcass up the stairs.

Just as I reached the second-floor landing, Rosa

opened her door and gaped at me. "What happened to you?"

I didn't feel like answering any questions, but my kid sister insisted that I come into her charming apartment so she could look at the bruise forming on my jaw and my slightly swollen nose. I told her the whole story while she brewed me a cup of chamomile tea.

"Good Lord, what will Ma say when she finds out?" Rosa's eyes were wide. I couldn't tell if she was impressed or alarmed or both. I didn't care. I just wanted to crawl into my bed, pull my freshly laundered white sheets and Marine-issue olive drab woolen blanket up around my chin, and sink into slumberland.

"Since Ma doesn't know about this, let's not tell her. You think the first thing I'd do after being mugged is call Ma and give her a heart attack?" I tried to sound severe as I warned her, "And if you and I keep this little incident to ourselves—that includes not telling the rest of the family—maybe we can spare her that cardiac arrest, okay? Otherwise she will be pestering yours truly to take secretarial classes."

Rosa nodded silently. I thanked her for the tea and went up to my own not-quite-so-charming apartment to sleep it off.

On Saturday morning, I went back to the office to finish up some paperwork on the Leone insurance claims. But first, I settled back with the Boston *Globe* and a cup of coffee. Although the headlines on the third page were small, they screamed at me: RETIRED COP MUGGED, KILLED. POLICE SEARCH FOR SUSPECT.

My jaw would have dropped open if it hadn't been so sore. I settled for sitting on the edge of my seat. According to the article, Tom Grady had been drinking at a pub in Boston's Combat Zone. He left a little after one last night. Several hours later, two policemen on a routine

round found his body half a block away near a
Dumpster. He'd been knifed. I shuddered as I remembered that on that same night, I'd been mugged at knifepoint. The Combat Zone was only about a mile away
from Faneuil Hall.

It didn't seem possible that there was a connection, but
guilt washed over me just the same. If only I'd shot my
attacker's leg out from under him. If only I'd run faster
and caught up with the mugger, beating him to a pulp
before turning him over to the cops. If only I'd taken the
knife away instead of letting him recover it. Maybe
Grady would be alive today. But I had no idea if my
mugger was Grady's murderer. It seemed too pat, so I
tried to shake off the feeling that my mugging was connected to Tom Grady's death.

Something elusive tugged at my memory. I tried to
concentrate on it, but it slipped away. Frustrated, I filed
the uneasy feeling away until I had more time to think it
over. In the meantime, to ease my conscience, I decided
to ask a few questions. And I'd start with someone who
was in charge of the investigation, someone who was
quoted in the article. I doubted that anyone on the case
was going to be around over the weekend, but I could at
least leave a message for the detective in charge, Lee Randolph, to call me.

## ♣ Chapter 7

On Sunday, I woke up to an urgent pounding on the door. My clock read five minutes before noon. Fumbling for my ratty secondhand Pendleton wool robe, I fell out of bed, stumbled to the door, and opened it. Rosa stood in the hall, dressed in new jeans, an oversize blouse, and a blazer—which meant only one thing.

"Oh, no," I groaned. "We have to go to Ma's today, right?" Ma lived in Malden—close enough to expect her children to visit frequently but blessedly far enough away to have only infrequent bus service into Boston.

Rosa grinned and pushed her way past me. "Don't worry, Sarge. Get in the shower while I make the coffee."

I hadn't looked in the mirror yet to see how badly bruised I still was from the other night's little misadventure, but when I touched my jaw, it felt very tender. I went into the bathroom and examined my face in the mirror. Both my jaw and nose had turned a lovely black and blue.

Twenty minutes later, I was sprawled on the sofa, my hands wrapped around a steaming mug of strong coffee. My head was still buzzing from waking up so unceremoniously.

Ever since I left the Marines, I've been going back to my old habits—waking up slowly is one of them. When I was still incarcerated in the service, we'd have to be up by six A.M. hitting the showers instead of hitting the snooze alarm for that extra ten-minute sleep fix.

Rosa was staring at me from the other end of the couch.

"What?" I asked.

She leaned forward and scrutinized my face. "It seems to be fading," she said, reaching out and touching my nose.

"Ouch!" I yelped, drawing back from her touch.

"You can't hide that from Ma," Rosa said darkly.

I sighed. "You're right," I replied, adding cheerfully, "and since I can't hide it from Ma, then I guess I'll be missing Sunday dinner with the family."

"Angie!" Rosa gasped at the thought. Even though she didn't get along with our mother, she still had familial responsibility deeply ingrained in her: family above all else. I, on the other hand, had managed to escape the apron strings altogether. While I loved my family, Ma especially, I didn't feel that sense of duty that was the be-all-and-end-all for most of the Matelli clan.

"Tell her I caught a cold or something," I suggested. Rosa frowned. "Please, sis. I can't go there looking like this." I gestured to my face and tried to look as pathetic as possible.

Reluctantly, Rosa agreed to make my excuses for me. She also agreed to bring some leftovers home. "Especially those stuffed artichokes of hers," I said eagerly. "Frankly, I sure would welcome any of Ma's home cooking." Before Rosa left, I gave her a key to the downstairs apartment to pass on to our older, more irresponsible sister, Sophia.

I spent most of the day pacing back and forth in my

apartment. I didn't feel right leaving my home, because of the stares I'd get—no woman can go out in public with a face like mine and not expect to be handed the number of a battered women's shelter by everyone she encounters. So I watched a couple of bad horror movies in the afternoon, but mostly I was distracted by Tom Grady's death. It felt strange to realize that Tom Grady was still owed two days' worth of investigation, which was what I planned to give him. And it felt stranger still when I reminded myself that my client was a corpse.

On Monday morning, I decided not to phone Detective Randolph. Instead, I took the T over to Arlington Street and walked briskly over to the police station on Berkeley Street. I'd never been inside, but I'd always admired the architecture, a huge white Gothic structure right out of the days of Jack the Ripper. While the exterior looked like a castle straight out of my worst nightmare, the interior was depressingly like a police station, with a cracked and grubby tile floor, pale green walls, and the smell of fear permeating every nook and cranny. A mesh cage window blocked off free entry into the building. The desk sergeant was stationed there to take any citizens' complaints and to direct people with appointments through the door.

The clientele was equally depressing. Several hookers with bored expressions were being escorted by tired-looking plainclothesmen through an unmarked security door that buzzed every time someone entered. A sweaty, tubby little man with a nervous tic emerged from it a few moments later. He paused to peer around the lobby, then scurried out of the entrance as if afraid someone was following him. I pegged him as a police informant who had been hauled in on a bust he'd helped arrange. Maybe I was wrong, but I've always believed you can tell a lot about a person by reading his facial expressions and gestures.

The desk sergeant pointed to me and said, "You got a complaint or an appointment?"

I stated my business and gave him Detective Randolph's name. He made a phone call to confirm that the detective was in and available, then pointed to the security door and buzzed me in.

The first thing I noticed about Detective Lee Randolph was his whimsical tie; it had little yellow whales swimming around on a dark blue background. When I took my eyes off the tie and examined the man, I realized that Randolph was an impressive-looking guy, lean and lanky, over six feet tall with a moon face, a mop of sandy curls, and mild eyes behind wire-rimmed glasses that were straight out of the sixties. He looked so laid back that I had to resist the urge to give him the peace sign.

He guided me into an empty room, one of those interrogation rooms from TV cop shows where one cop beats the crap out of the suspect while his partner asks the suspect if he wants cream in his coffee.

"I don't usually have attractive young ladies drop by unexpectedly," Randolph said with a smile as he pulled a chair out for me to sit in. "Especially when it involves murder."

I sat and watched him pull another chair out and turn it around. Although I'd originally pegged him as the guy who got coffee for the suspect, my impression of him altered when he straddled the chair and leaned toward me. There was a determined glint in his eye as he asked, "Now, what did you say your name was?"

I took a business card out of my coat pocket and handed it to him. He studied it as I launched into an account of my business with Tom Grady.

"As you can see by my card," I began, "I'm a private

investigator. For starters, I'd like to know what the status of Tom Grady's death is around here. Have you concluded your investigation?"

"Tom Grady?" Randolph looked up sharply. "He's the fellow who was murdered on Friday night, eh?" The detective ran a hand over his hair. "Normally I wouldn't give out information about an ongoing investigation, but most of the information is available to the public. We have no reason to believe Mr. Grady's death was connected to anything other than the mugging. Of course, the case isn't officially closed, but we don't hold out much hope of catching the killer." He clasped his hands together and looked down at them as he continued, "Of course, the fact that he's a retired policeman makes us look all the harder for a suspect." He shook his head and looked up at me. "But frankly, Miss Matelli, I don't think this case is going to be solved. It looks like the mugger panicked and stabbed his victim. We've combed the area for witnesses, but no one admits to seeing anything. Do you have any information that might lead us to a suspect?"

I said, "I worked for Grady the week before he was killed."

"Doing what?"

"Following someone, investigating a background."

Randolph looked a bit put out as he asked, "Can you be more specific?" I didn't blame him. At the moment, I was indecisive about how much to tell him. Should I lay the whole case out for him, names and all, or should I tell him just enough to justify my concern about being mugged on the same night Grady was killed?

Randolph spoke up again. "What does your work for Tom Grady have to do with his murder?"

"I'm not sure, but I have this feeling that there's a connection between Grady's murder and the fact that I was mugged earlier on the same night." There. I'd laid my doubts out in front of him.

Detective Randolph leaned forward and peered at my face. "Is that how you got that bruised jaw?"

I involuntarily reached up as if to make sure the bruise was still there. I had inspected it this morning in the bathroom mirror and it had faded from purple to a greenish yellow, but it still ached a bit. "Yeah," I said. "My face got in the way of his fist."

The detective tried to suppress a smile, and succeeded only in frowning. "Where were you mugged?"

"Near Faneuil Hall on Friday night between ten and ten-thirty."

"And what would this have to do with the work you did for Mr. Grady?" He stared at me and pointed out, "Lots of people get mugged in Boston on a Friday night."

"That's true, but suppose it was the same mugger—he certainly had enough time to find Tom Grady after he tried to mug me." After a moment's thought, I added, "And now that I think about it, I got the impression that it wasn't an ordinary mugger. That I might have ended up like Grady."

"Why didn't you?"

"End up like my client?" I asked. Randolph nodded. He was sitting up straight, as if he were getting interested in the case again. I said, "I fought back and got lucky, unlike Tom Grady."

Randolph said nothing, preferring to let me continue.

I explained, "It was on Salt Street, one of the little side streets that go through to Merchants Row. I was taking a shortcut to the T and he stepped out, put a knife to my throat, and demanded my shoulder bag."

"You gave it to him?"

I hesitated, wondering if it would be smart to mention

the gun in my bag. I decided to leave it out of my recounting. "The strap caught on a shoulder button on my jacket. I told him to let up on the knife a bit so I could pull it free. He stepped back slightly, leaving me enough room to jab my elbow in his solar plexus."

"You know, it's not wise to turn on your attacker unless you know what you're doing. You take a women's defense class or something?" Detective Randolph narrowed his eyes, obviously reevaluating his assessment of me.

I smiled and said, "Yeah. On Parris Island, South Carolina."

Randolph's raised eyebrows told me that he knew what I was talking about. "Ex-Marine, huh? I figured you'd been in the service when you walked in here."

I nodded. No explanation was necessary. I had that precise walk that comes with eight years in the military.

"Where did you serve?" he asked.

"Japan. California. Other places."

"Nam here," he replied. We nodded cautiously, aware that we had a bond, although not a terribly pleasant one for him. I had managed to escape the Vietnam experience. I was only nine or ten years old at the time. Detective Randolph was about ten years my senior. He probably caught the tail end of the draft.

I had even managed to evade the Gulf War. My superior officers had decided that I would be more useful on the Mexican border, looking for contraband.

I steered back to the subject of Tom Grady. "Anyway, we fought, he dropped the knife, I, uh"—I caught myself before mentioning my gun—"stepped back. I thought he was down, knocked out maybe, and I was just about to get some help when he struggled up, grabbed his knife, and ran away."

"And you mentioned earlier that this was between ten and ten-thirty?" he asked.

I nodded. "I looked at my watch when I reached the marketplace, after I'd lost him."

"Why didn't you report it before now?"

"There didn't seem to be any point that night. The mugger didn't get my purse and the only things I got were these matching souvenirs on my nose and jaw. The funny thing is—" I stopped to figure out how to put this in words, "I didn't feel that he tried hard enough to get my purse. I felt all along that it was just an excuse. I mean, he stepped back instead of using the knife to slice through the strap." I saw Detective Randolph's quizzical look and hastily added, "Not that I'm complaining, but it just seemed strange. If he really was a mugger, wouldn't he have done that? He seemed more intent on harming me."

He looked amused for a moment, then serious. "As a policeman, I have to tell you that you should have reported it that night. We might have combed the area and caught him. But ex-Marine to ex-Marine, I don't think the report would have done a damn thing." The detective pulled out a notebook and pencil. "Why don't I take down a description of this mugger of yours. If we find him and you can identify him in a lineup, we can question him about Tom Grady's murder."

I nodded and told him as much as I could about my attacker. Unfortunately, it had been dark and I had spent most of my time feeling his hot breath on my neck or struggling with him. I gave Randolph the spare details such as approximate height, weight, hair color and length, clean-shaven face, and the clothes he was wearing. I couldn't give Randolph any identifying scars or tattoos, shape of the nose or mouth, whether his ears stuck out, if his feet were huge, or whether his low raspy voice was normal or affected. When I finished, he sighed and said, "Well, it's not much to go on, but I'll make sure this description gets out. Maybe he'll mug someone else in the meantime and we'll get a matching description with more details."

"As long as the victim isn't knifed like Tom Grady was," I reminded him. The interview was formally over. I got up, we shook hands, promised to keep each other informed on anything that turned up, then I left.

As I walked to the T, I turned over what Randolph had told me, which wasn't much. I was no more sure of what I was going to do next than was Detective Randolph. But I knew that I had to do something. I still felt that Grady's murder and my mugging were linked, and until proven wrong, I would pursue this case. Maybe it's just that I hate being punched in the jaw.

# ♣ Chapter 8

Tom Grady was to be buried out in Dorchester the next day. When Tuesday dawned, no one could have asked for a colder, wetter, more miserable day for a funeral. The idea of attending Grady's funeral was not as uncomfortable for me as some of the funerals I'd attended as a child. Of course, being part of a large Italian family, I was thoroughly familiar with funerals and weddings. My mother had required her family to attend any event that involved even the most distant relation. I had been to the funerals of relatives I'd never even met. At least I had met and talked with Tom Grady.

When I got up that morning, I opened my closet. I hadn't realized until then that I had very little in the way of civilian clothes. I didn't think fatigues would be suitable, nor my dress uniform. Just about everything else in the closet was way out of date. I was about to settle on a slate gray blouse with my dressy black jeans when I spied something in the corner. I pulled it out and held it up. It was a black dress, just what I needed! It was only slightly out of date—I had bought it in the late seventies for my prom. I never made it to what was supposed to be the most unforgettable night of my high school years. But that's another story.

I shook the dress out. It was a little too flashy—a fake rose on the waist and flounces on the shoulders that looked like wings—but a pair of scissors took care of those problems. When I was finished, the dress looked good enough to pass inspection at a funeral, especially after I paired it with a basic black wool blazer.

Accessories were another matter. I found a pair of plain black pumps, but couldn't find one pair of nylons in the entire apartment. So I did what any self-respecting, but desperate, female private investigator would do in my case: I used my master key to get into Rosa's apartment and rummaged through her lingerie drawer until I came upon a pair of panty hose with no runs in them. Before I left her apartment, I peeked in her refrigerator to see if she'd brought anything back from Sunday dinner for me. Sure enough, there was a care package with stuffed artichokes, ravioli with marinara sauce, and a couple of other goodies. I gathered everything together and left a note of thanks pinned to her refrigerator, then went back up to my apartment.

Standing in front of the full-length mirror I'd had installed on my bedroom closet, I inspected myself carefully. I was pleased with the results. I looked almost professional. The panty hose were a bit too small (weren't they always?) and I had to readjust them at the crotch so I couldn't look knock-kneed. I wasn't dressed in anything as snazzy as Anne Klein, but I looked respectable. People wouldn't point me out in a crowd and laugh. I locked up the apartment, got in my car, and headed for Dorchester.

His funeral was held in a small cathedral and was well attended. Aside from the usual family members, there were dozens of policemen and retired policemen in dress uniform to send off one of their own.

I almost didn't recognize ginger-haired Brian Scanlon,

who was sitting in one of the front pews. The last time I saw him, he had been wearing work clothes. Today, he wore a black suit, blue-striped shirt, and a navy tie. I thought there would be very little chance that he would recognize me. It wasn't as if I'd climbed onto the bar at the Shandy and sung "Danny Boy" at the top of my lungs or anything like that. Unless Sheilah's boyfriend was paranoid, I didn't think he would even give me a second glance. Unless he had something to do with my mugging.

The woman sitting next to Scanlon had to be Sheilah Grady. A model-thin woman with classic upturned nose, she had the dark, wavy hair and translucent skin that was usually associated with the "black Irish." She wore a simple black long-sleeved wool dress and veil, a damp hankie in her hand. Everyone who ventured up to the casket to pay their last respects would stop for a moment and talk to her before taking their seats.

I've never been too crazy about viewing dead bodies, even if they're dressed up in a fancy coffin, so I decided to wait in a pew. My intention was to approach Sheilah when the funeral was over. The priest who gave the mass went on for close to an hour, which was typical of any Catholic ceremony. There was a lot of standing and kneeling and sitting, reciting and praying and genuflecting, and, of course, the ever popular transubstantiation, which I decided to skip. I would have felt like an imposter receiving the wafer.

Don't get me wrong—I grew up Catholic. Even though I stopped attending Sunday mass when I went into the Marines, I still write "Catholic" on any form that asks me to state my religion. But I am what many people politely call a "lapsed Catholic."

After the ceremony, Sheilah stood near the church door to thank everyone for attending, as they left. I watched the line of people move slowly toward the exit and thought I caught a glimpse of Seamus McRaney and Scanlon's friend Mike, but I couldn't be sure. I brought up the rear of the line, thus assuring that I would be the last to leave.

Brian Scanlon had been called away to help carry the casket to the hearse. Sheilah turned to me and held out her hand, her eyes scanning my face for something familiar, some point of reference to grasp that would help her remember my name.

I saved her the embarrassment by introducing myself as I shook her hand. "Angela Matelli. I did some work for your father. I was terribly sorry to hear about his death."

"Miss Matelli," she repeated, the grief evident in her eyes. "The name sounds familiar, but I can't quite place it." Of course, we both knew that she was just being polite.

I figured there wasn't any reason to be coy about my profession. So I said, "I'm a private investigator."

I thought I detected a glint of recognition in her eyes, but it could have just been uncried tears. She nodded solemnly.

I continued, "I didn't know your father well, but I was still shocked and saddened by the news."

She appeared to have collected herself. "What did my father need with a private investigator?" she asked, cocking her head in a gesture of polite interest.

I hesitated. I could not divulge this information to her, even if she was related. It was one thing to cooperate with the police by giving them the information—my client was dead and coincidentally I had been attacked in the same manner on the same night as Tom Grady. If I hadn't been assaulted, I don't know if I would have gone to the police with information regarding my business with

Grady. But Sheilah appeared to be asking out of curiosity, and since her father's business had involved his daughter's boyfriend, I didn't think it would be a good idea for me to divulge the facts.

So I smiled and said, "I'm really sorry, Miss Grady. That's privileged information. I wish I could tell you, but I don't think it's anything vital for you to know."

Sheilah Grady frowned, then nodded. "It doesn't matter anyway, Miss Matelli. I think I already know what you were supposed to be doing for my father." Her weary eyes met mine and she added, "You see, a few hours before he was killed, Dad and I had a big blowout over Brian."

I didn't know if this was going anywhere, so I just said, "Well, again, my condolences." I started to move away when she called after me.

"Miss Matelli!" I turned around and came back. Sheilah Grady's eyes burned bright, almost feverish. She said, "Would it be possible—can I set up an appointment to visit you tomorrow?"

We were interrupted by Brian Scanlon. He came up the church steps and slipped a hand under Sheilah's elbow. "Honey, we're ready to go now." He turned to look at me with open curiosity.

Sheilah introduced me. "This is Angela Matelli," she said, gesturing to me, then leaned against him. "Angela, this is Brian Scanlon, my support system through all of this."

I smiled and we shook hands, murmuring niceties to each other.

"Did you know Sheilah's father well, Miss Matelli?" Brian asked.

*Oh boy,* I thought, *how do I handle this one?* Sheilah was being no help in letting me know how honest I should be in front of him. I opted for the neutral approach until I could get more information from her. "I'd only known him for a short time," I replied, "but I came to really like him." It was honest, anyway.

Although he seemed satisfied outwardly, I got the feeling that Brian's sharp eyes didn't miss a trick. He was studying me for any outward signs that I wasn't what I appeared to be. He couldn't have made it more obvious to me that he was an ex-con. That look of distrust upon first meeting someone in a tragic but innocuous situation like this one was a dead giveaway.

"Well, we've got to go," he said to Sheilah, then turned to me. "It was nice meeting you."

I nodded and stared after them.

Suddenly Sheilah leaned over to Brian and whispered something in his ear. He nodded and she broke away from him, turning to jog up the steps toward me. When she got close enough, she asked in a low voice, "Would ten o'clock tomorrow morning be a good time for you?"

"Fine," I replied. "I'm free then." *I'm free until the oceans run dry,* I thought as I watched the hearse, then Brian and Sheilah's limousine, pull away from the curb.

Sheilah Grady arrived at my office on the dot of ten o'clock on Wednesday morning. Punctuality must have been her middle name.

"Would you like a cup of coffee?" I asked as she seated herself across from me.

"Yes, that would be nice." She dropped her purse on the floor. Today she wore a dark gray pinstripe blazer and skirt, the type of outfit that young up-and-coming executives wear. Since she worked at Shamrock Imports as a shipping clerk, I wondered why she was wearing such a stylish outfit to a warehouse. Maybe she was wearing it to mourn her father.

I reached down into the deli bag and brought out two

coffees I'd picked up this morning on my way in.

"Would you like regular or black?" For some bizarre reason, East Coasters thought of "regular" coffee as having cream in it. You had to specify if you wanted black coffee. Although I'd lived here most of my life, I still didn't understand the reasoning behind it. I just had to consider it one of those little quirks that sets the East Coast apart from the rest of the world.

I'd ordered one of each, a regular and a black, because I wasn't particular about how I drank my deli coffee. It tasted good either way.

She chose the regular and, as she reached for it, her eyes scanned my office. "You should consider getting a coffee machine. You wouldn't have to run out for deli coffee." I felt compelled to explain.

"I just moved in here a few weeks ago," I muttered apologetically. "I haven't had much time to furnish it with all the comforts yet." Besides, I made a lousy cup of coffee.

Sheilah Grady sipped her coffee, then said, "You don't have to apologize, Miss Matelli. I think it's very nice of you to go to all this trouble."

She seemed reluctant to get down to business. However, I was curious to know what she needed to see me about, so I took the direct approach.

"What can I do for you, Miss Grady?"

She hesitated before saying, "Can we dispense with the formalities? I prefer to be called Sheilah."

I nodded and responded, "Angela." I leaned forward and said once again, "Okay, Sheilah. Now that we're on a first-name basis, can you give me a hint as to why you think you need my services?" I've found that sometimes it was best to be blunt with people who were reluctant to get to the point.

She took a deep breath and said, "I want to hire you to investigate my father's death."

I pushed my chair back from the desk. I shouldn't have been surprised, of course. Her dad had been killed by a mugger and she wanted justice. I just wasn't sure there was much of a trail anymore. Anything at the crime scene had been found by the police already, bagged, tagged, and, after the lab went over it and the report was written, tucked away in a locker.

My face must have betrayed my skepticism, because Sheilah quickly added, "Oh, I know the police have done everything in their power to catch the mugger who killed him, even more than they would have done if he hadn't been one of them. But I think it would take some of the burden off of them if they knew I had hired someone full-time to look into his death. I haven't been able to sleep since Daddy died. . . ." she trailed off, dug a handkerchief out of her purse, and dabbed at her eyes.

"What exactly do you want me to do?" I asked, starting to lose my patience. I know I should have been more sympathetic, but I wanted her to get right to the point. "You know the police have only had a few days to investigate."

She dropped the hankie back into her bag and said, "But the trail is growing colder every day. There has to be someone out there who witnessed something before or after Dad's murder. The police have already asked around the murder scene and haven't come up with any witnesses. I know that they'll slack off of this case soon. I'm not convinced it was just a mugging gone wrong. I'd feel better knowing that someone is on the case full-time, looking for new leads."

I perked up, wondering if she knew about my experience that same night, or whether there was some new information here. "Why aren't you convinced that it was just a mugging?" I asked.

"Well, yesterday I told you that we had a big fight before he went out that night. After we fought, he got a phone call that he took in his study, and when he hung up, he seemed upset." She paused.

I asked, "What time was this?"

"About nine."

"Maybe you'd better start from the beginning. Tell me everything, including what may seem to you to be unimportant details." I leaned back in my chair, prepared to listen to everything she had to say and take notes of things that seemed important, or things that at least needed to be questioned.

Sheilah thought a moment, then nodded. "I usually come over on Friday evenings to cook dinner for him. Brian used to come over, too, but Dad never liked him to begin with. Lately, he'd pick fights with Brian over everything, from religion to politics to whether Brian had buttered his bread correctly. So Brian had begun to stay away.

"I cooked Dad's favorite dish, stuffed cabbage. Mother taught me how to make it before she died. After dinner, we watched a rented movie and then we talked a bit. I noticed that he was more introspective that night than usual. Later, he excused himself and went into the study to make a call. I couldn't hear what he said, but from the tone of his voice, he sounded pretty angry."

I asked, "You didn't hear anything that he said?"

She hesitated. Finally Sheilah replied, "Actually, I was thirsty, so I got up and went into the kitchen. I had to pass the study door, which was ajar, and I caught the tail end of the conversation. Dad was saying, 'You'd better be on time.' Then he hung up.

"We didn't fight right away. I noticed that he kept

looking at his watch and pacing the living room, which meant that he was very agitated about something. Then, out of the blue, he started saying terrible things about Brian."

I interrupted her again. "What sort of things?"

"He told me that Brian was a terrorist, that he was a member of some sort of radical political organization. When I asked him what he was talking about, he said, 'The ILAP.' I told him that I belonged to that organization and that we weren't radical, unless you considered liberating politically oppressed prisoners revolutionary."

For the second time during this meeting with Sheilah Grady, I was taken by surprise. I had witnessed Brian Scanlon's meeting with Seamus McRaney over a week ago, and after finding out that McRaney's organization was allegedly a front for terrorist activities, I had thought that an ex-con like Scanlon, a political radical, might be involved in a deal with McRaney. But with Sheilah now in the ILAP picture, with everything out in the open, I wondered if it might just be what it appeared to be—innocent.

Of course, it was possible that Scanlon and McRaney were meeting to discuss mutual terrorist interests without Sheilah's knowledge. Could this be the information Tom Grady had wanted me to find out? If so, he certainly didn't give me much to go on. And he refused my services at a point when I could have dug deeper into the case.

I pulled my wandering attention back to Sheilah. She was sitting there, dabbing at her eyes with a crumpled tissue.

I feigned ignorance and asked, "Did your father just suggest these things, or did he have proof to go with his accusations?"

She shifted in her chair and replied, "Daddy didn't have proof, but he thought the founder of ILAP, Seamus

McRaney, used his organization as a front for terrorism. Aidan McRaney, Seamus's father, had been a member of the IRA. There's been no connection made that Seamus is an IRA sympathizer. The opposite is true—he's spoken out against the IRA, condemning their use of force. I think the conservatives are afraid of change, so they attack Seamus from the other side. He's caught in the middle, hated by the IRA for speaking out against them, and feared by the old guard."

I continued my line of questioning. "So did your father accuse you as well? I mean, if he was afraid your boyfriend was involved in something unsavory, wouldn't he suspect you of the same thing?"

She shook her head and reluctantly said, "No. Brian is an ex-con."

I raised my eyebrows slightly to show I was surprised when, in fact, I was not.

She continued, "He was arrested and thrown in jail for conspiracy and planting a bomb. But that was back in the early seventies. He did his time, fifteen years of an eighteen-year sentence." She shook her head mournfully. "Brian had plenty of years to think about what he'd done back in college. In the late sixties, he and several of his friends were influenced by what the Weathermen were doing in Chicago."

"You mean the Days of Rage protests?" I asked. I *am* counterculturally literate.

She nodded, looking properly impressed with my knowledge of the sixties. "Well, Brian had been organizing several antiwar protests, but felt frustrated by the lack of results. He wanted to make a difference. So when the Weathermen made headlines in 1969 with their violent demonstration during the trial of the Chicago Seven, Brian organized a similar group here in Boston. He called his group Storm D, which stood for Students Tired of RandoM Death."

I had heard of the organization. I made a face. She shrugged in response and went on to explain, "He was just interested in ending the war. He adopted the Weathermen's belief that by bringing a piece of the war home, more people would be willing to stand up against what was happening in Vietnam."

I wanted to gauge her reaction to an attack against Brian Scanlon, so I said, "In other words, he was part of a terrorist group."

Her lips tightened a little bit, but she reined in her feelings pretty well. "I wouldn't call it a terrorist group, but I'd say their beliefs got a little out of hand. Choosing the Weathermen as idols probably wasn't the brightest thing Brian's ever done. Besides, he's done his time. He's paid, he's out, we're in love, and we both belong to the ILAP." She looked away and added, "I guess Brian felt he had to continue doing something political, and prisoners' rights—political prisoners' rights, that is—seemed to be the way to put something good back into the system."

I nodded, silent. I thought it unwise to bring up my own suspicions. Besides, we'd gotten way off track.

"So after your father left, what did you do?" I asked, hoping that it didn't sound too obvious. I was checking up on her alibi.

"Oh, cleaned up the dishes, then went home. Brian was waiting for me," she said blithely. "He'd rented some movies and we stayed in the rest of the night."

Then she looked straight at me and said, "So will you look into my father's death? I know about the trail being cold and all, but it sure would make me feel better."

I said, "Sure. I'll see what I can do for you. But if I don't come up with anything promising in, say, three days, I'll let you know. I don't want you to waste your money."

She took out her checkbook, my favorite part of a potential client interview, and handed me a check, already signed, dated, and with a several nice, round zeros after a one. Nice to know she was so prepared. "Will this be enough?"

I kept a poker face as I glanced at the check to watch the ink dry. "This will do fine," I said. "You will get a refund of whatever is left after expenses, if I don't come up with anything. Is there anyplace you'd like me to start?"

She hesitated before asking, "Where would you suggest?"

I turned it over for a minute in my mind, then said, "Does his house still have a seal on it?"

"No. The police did a thorough search, but came up empty." She dug in her purse, produced a set of keys, and handed them to me.

"I'll probably go over the place anyway," I explained, "looking for some clue as to who he could have called before you had an argument. I'll also be looking for witnesses down at the bar where he . . ." I trailed off, not being able to think of a nice phrase, then finished up with, "was drinking before he left."

She stood up. "Do you need anything else?"

I thought a moment, then replied, "If you have a photo of your father, that would be a great help, especially if I'm going to be looking for witnesses down in the Zone."

She pulled out her wallet and flipped through the plastic card section of it until she produced a head shot of her dad. I studied it, then set it aside with the house keys.

"I just want to let you know again how sorry I am about your father. . . ."

She nodded, an impassive look on her face. "Thank

you. He was a good father and I'll miss him. When should I expect a report from you?"

"I'll get in touch with you at the end of every day, if you want."

"That will be fine." She hesitated before leaving, and asked, "Angela, could you satisfy my curiosity?"

"If I can."

"I think I know what my father hired you to do." Then she asked softly, "Did you find anything?"

*How much does she know?* I thought. *Should I tell her about my mugging the night Tom Grady was killed?* There was a chance that Grady threatened Brian Scanlon with some information he'd discovered—maybe he guessed what activities Brian Scanlon was involved in and was killed for it. I didn't know yet, but I knew it wouldn't be a good idea to tell his daughter because it would put her in a dangerous position. Knowledge may be power, but it can also be deadly.

Instead, I replied, "Nothing you didn't already know."

# ♣ Chapter 9

$\mathcal{B}$efore I began investigating Tom Grady's death, I phoned Detective Randolph to let him know that Sheilah Grady had hired me. Knowing how much law officers love private investigators muscling in on their territory, I was prepared for a hostile response. Instead, Randolph sounded almost relieved.

"I usually don't work well with private investigators," he said. "But after talking to you the other day, I think you're on the level."

Being a Marine, or even an ex-Marine, is like being a member of an exclusive club. "Oh, you can trust me," I heard myself say. I sounded like an eager puppy trying to please her master. Mentally, I hit myself smartly on the nose with an imaginary rolled-up newspaper.

Meanwhile, Detective Randolph was still trying to justify why he was acting as my personal fountain of information. I knew he was slightly uncomfortable with this working situation, despite the fact that I was a fellow ex-Marine. I wasn't sure if he was trying to convince me or himself.

"You did come to me the other day with information that you felt was connected to Tom Grady's case."

"Has there been—" I started to ask how the case was coming along, but he answered before I could finish.

"Nothing has come of the investigation yet," he said. "There was so little to go on. I guess we'll never know what we missed."

"Did you find anything at Tom Grady's home?" I asked.

"There wasn't anything in there that we could connect with his death," he replied. "Unless you come up with something, we may never find the killer. I hate to admit defeat, especially when the murder victim is a fellow cop. We're still looking, but I have a mountain of new cases that have just come in and we can't spare any more time on this line of inquiry."

As we were winding up our conversation, I took a chance and asked, "Why are you really helping me? I know that you said you'd taken a liking to me and all, but there has to be more to it than that."

"The case is unofficially closed," Randolph admitted. "And as a private investigator licensed by the state, you know that you're expected by law to turn over any concrete evidence of foul play. You will contact me immediately, won't you?"

"I'll keep you apprised of my progress," I assured him in my best "military speak." Probably one of the most valuable resources a private investigator can have is the confidence of someone on the police force. I just lucked out and got a homicide detective on my first case.

After I thanked him and hung up, I considered everything I had learned. It was hard to determine where to start. There weren't very many leads and I had to choose one to start with. I took a quarter from the extra change I kept in my desk drawer and tossed it. Heads, I would start with a search of Grady's house. Tails, I'd start looking for witnesses in the area of Grady's murder. The latter choice would mean spending a lot of time in the Combat Zone, Boston's very own den of iniquity. It was a much smaller den these days now that Chinatown was gradually taking over the area. On the night of his death, Grady had been drinking at the Wild Irish Rose Pub until midnight. His body was found at three in the morning behind a garbage Dumpster, just half a block away from the pub. Let's just say I was rooting for heads. The quarter came up tails. You win some, you lose some.

Before I left my office, I put Grady's photo in my wallet with the other photos of my family. I thought about taking my gun—the Zone is no place for a woman to be hanging around unless she's a working girl—but it was daylight. I left it in the drawer.

I took the T down to the Park Street Station, then walked up Winter Street to Washington. I always know when I've crossed into the Combat Zone by the sudden rise in the number of slimy-looking men.

Every once in a while, some well-meaning citizen decides it's time to clean up our fair city. The first thing on their agenda is to clean up the high-crime sectors. But the Combat Zone is like dried blood set in fabric; it has been through the wash many times, but it will never go away.

Somewhere along the line, the advocates realize that they've been getting nowhere—like hamsters on a wheel—so they turn their attention to some easier, equally good cause like trying to get heavy metal albums banned because they played an album backward and could swear they heard "All hail Satan."

Bar after bar after bar lined Washington Street with signs that ranged from FEATURING TOPLESS COLLEGE GIRLS to ALL NUDE REVUE. The denizens of the area wander the streets in the daytime like vampires who have lost their coffins. And like Count Dracula, they're in their element at night.

I stopped in front of the Wild Irish Rose Pub and looked around. Turning south on Washington, I came to the Dumpster where Grady was found. It was outside another bar called the Exchange. I didn't have to go inside to know what type of bar it was.

I went back to the Wild Irish Rose and went inside the dimly lit bar. A soccer match was playing on a black and white television in a corner behind the bar. The volume was loud, almost earsplitting. The air was stale with cigarette smoke. Through the haze, I detected the distinctly strong smell of a cigar. Behind the counter, the bartender was rubbing down the bar with a dirty rag. A stubby stogie was jammed between his teeth. He eyed me in a disinterested way.

"What can I getcha?" he asked gruffly. He stopped what he was doing, pulled the cigar out of his mouth, and coughed.

I slipped onto a creaky stool and replied, "I'll have a beer on tap."

He nodded, clamped his teeth around the burning cigar, and grabbed a mug, turning around to pull the beer tap.

I took in the atmosphere while I was waiting. There were quite a few patrons in the pub; most of them looked like they were on pensions or disability. Several grizzled old barflies sat at the other end of the bar and watched me covertly as they sipped their beer.

My beer was placed in front of me and I dug into my pocket to pay for it.

"You just in the neighborhood?" the bartender asked me. He'd taken his cigar out of his mouth to cough again.

I smiled and paid him for the beer. "Actually, no. I'm interested in the murder that happened down here a few days ago. Last Friday, to be exact."

He frowned, eyeing me like I was a tourist who likes to

go slumming where murders happen. Or worse, I could be a journalist. I quickly disillusioned him.

"I'm a private investigator working for the daughter of the murder victim." I pulled my wallet out and showed him my business card and driver's license. He didn't look impressed.

Now, I know that in the movies and books, private detectives usually try to elicit information without revealing their identities. A certain amount of lying is necessary for someone in my profession—if the circumstances warrant it. But this didn't appear to be the type of situation where I needed to invent a false name and reason for asking around. So I'd told the truth. The bartender and most of the patrons had probably been thoroughly questioned by the police.

"I wasn't working that night," the barkeep said gruffly. He moved down the bar and ignored me.

I knew I was taking a chance, but I walked down the length of the bar until I got his attention again. He scowled, then reluctantly turned to me.

"I know you've probably had to deal with Boston's finest," I began, "but do you mind telling me if there's anyone around who could tell me about that night?"

"Yes, I mind. I've had enough problems with the little amount of publicity the *Globe* gave us," the taciturn bartender replied. "I don't need some private detective nosing around, looking for some sensational angle to Grady's death. It was a mugging, that's all."

"I take it Tom Grady was a good customer," I said. I'd decided to go ahead and ask, even though the barkeep seemed determined to make it as difficult as possible for me to do my job. Sometimes you have to overlook rude behavior in order to get the job done.

He watched me silently for what seemed like hours. In reality, it must have been only a few minutes. I met his eyes with a steady gaze of my own. It was turning into a test of wills.

Finally he looked down. "Look, miss—"

"Matelli," I replied. "Angela Matelli."

"Yeah, whatever. I only knew him a little. I work the early shift. I can't stop you from snoopin' around here unless you cause a commotion." He leaned toward me, pointed across the room, and said, "If you really want to know about Tom Grady, those are his drinking buddies over there."

My eyes followed the direction of his finger. Four men about Grady's age were gathered around a large round table. Three of them wore navy pea coats. Two of them wore black watch caps. One was bald, two had thick thatches of white hair, and the other still had his own bright red hair. All four had red-veined noses from drinking too much stout.

I walked over. Their eyes were bright—whether from drink or the fact that a woman was in their presence, it was hard to tell. I introduced myself and explained my business.

"Sit down, lass," the redheaded man said in a kindly tone laced in a thick brogue. He half rose from his seat, indicating an empty chair. I sat. He said, "I'm Paddy. Over here is Sean"—he gestured to the bald man, then pointed to the two white-haired men and added—"and these are the twins, Bertie and Bernie." Paddy wobbled back into his seat, his elbow jostling a near-empty pint of stout in front of him. It was then that I realized he was in his cups, as were the others. I wondered how many pints they'd already knocked back. It wasn't even noon yet.

"The bartender told me that you all knew Tom Grady," I began. "I understand that you were here the night he was killed."

"Aye, we knew Tommy well," Sean said with a light

Gaelic lilt, a wistful look in his eyes. "He was a good man and a good officer." He sighed and eyed his empty glass. "We've been drinking to his memory." Sean looked up at me and asked, "Would you care to join us?"

All four sets of eyes watched me guardedly. I smiled. "Sure. I'll even buy the next round."

I must have passed muster, because they suddenly broke into grins, nodding approval and calling to the bartender for a round of pints.

Paddy began. "I've known Grady since he walked a beat here in the Zone back in the old days."

I could tell this could be a long day of reminiscing and drinking, so I sped things up a bit. "Could you start with what happened that night when Tom Grady came in?"

"Well"—Paddy scratched his jaw as he tried to recall—"Tommy came in here around ten o'clock. He ordered his usual, a lager and lime. But he didn't join the fellas and me right away, like he usually did. The only reason he comes down to this pub anymore is to socialize with us. Instead, he sat at the bar and ignored us."

"Did you approach him? Did you talk to him at all?"

Sean nodded and joined in again. "One or the other of us went up to him several times and asked him to join us, but he wouldn't have any of it. I was the last one to try. I asked if anything was the matter, but Tommy just said, 'I'd like to join you boys later. But I've got something to take care of first.' So he kept to himself the rest of the time. And about eleven o'clock, he switched from his usual to Irish whiskey straight."

"Was that unusual?" I asked.

Up to this point, I'd been wondering if the twins ever spoke. But finally Bernie or Bertie—I had trouble keeping them straight—said, "Oh, yes. He usually stuck with lager and lime. He hated Guinness and rarely drank Irish whiskey unless it was a special occasion."

"It didn't seem to be a special occasion, though," Paddy said.

"How did he appear to you?" I asked. "Was he acting normally?"

Sean replied, "Well, he seemed a bit preoccupied." He looked around at his companions for confirmation. They nodded in unison.

"Preoccupied was what he was," said the other twin, Bertie or Bernie.

Paddy added, "I thought he looked upset, too."

"Aye," the three others replied. There followed a silence, all of them lifting their glasses in a silent toast. I joined them. My stout tasted bitter, warm, and dark. My second sip went down easier. It reminded me of molasses, but without the sugar. Like coffee, I could tell it might take a while to get used to stout. This was only the second time I'd ordered it.

I continued the inquiry. "Did Tom Grady do anything unusual during the evening, or was he approached by any strangers?"

They thought about this one. Three of them shook their heads, but a fourth, Bernie or Bertie, replied, "He kept looking at his watch, then glancing at the clock above the bar."

"Aye," said Sean, perking up a bit. "I noticed that, too. I'd clean forgotten that."

I tried again. "No strangers talked to him?"

All four men shook their heads. I sat in gloomy silence. This case had been dropped into my lap, the law was happy to see me working on the case, and I couldn't get a lead to save my life. Or solve Tom Grady's death. Maybe it was just a random mugging.

I went back over the facts of the night in question. His daughter had claimed that after dinner, her father had made a phone call in his study. She had heard him say on the phone, "You'd better be on time." Then his last hours were spent at the Wild Irish Rose Pub, drinking alone, and looking alternately at his watch and the clock over the bar.

Putting all these facts together, it seemed apparent to me that Tom Grady had had a meeting that night, an appointment that was never kept. Was the mysterious date male or female? How was I going to find the person who was supposed to meet Tom Grady at the Wild Irish Rose? My heart sank. I was going nowhere fast with this case.

I stayed for a time and listened to Paddy, Sean, Bernie, and Bertie regale me with stories about Tommy Grady in the "auld days" when he was just a young policeman on a beat here in the Zone. "Sean, do you remember that time all the dancers' G-strings disappeared from the stripper club down the street?" Paddy asked, by way of prompting Sean to tell the story.

"Ah, yes. He was a young man, just feelin' his oats back then." Sean chuckled. "He put more time and effort into tracking down that thief than any other man on the force."

"I heard tell he spent many a night going from club to club, drinking their drink and asking questions on his own time," Bertie or Bernie replied. "Never did catch the thief, but he had quite a few girls to date for a long time."

I chuckled appreciatively.

"Then there was the time Tommy had to take a man into the station who had been wandering around the streets without his pants on, singing 'Zip-a-Dee Doo-Dah,' " Paddy said, wiping a tear of laughter from his eye. "The thing is, no one phoned in to complain. The fellow'd been wanderin' around out there for near half an hour when Tommy ran across him."

By now I had a buzz on. Even though the story wasn't

that funny, I found myself laughing so hard my sides were hurting. I found enough breath to ask what I'd been curious about since meeting these four men. "Do any of you fellas know a retired cop by the name of Charlie Matelli?"

Everyone stopped laughing and looked at each other for a moment. I was afraid I'd said the wrong thing, but suddenly Sean broke out in a smile. "Do we know him! He was a right bugger, he was. We still see him at the monthly meetings of the Retired Policemen's Association."

"He's my uncle," I said with pride.

Bernie, who I now realized had a small mole by his left eyebrow, frowned slightly. "He was one of Tommy's partners, wasn't he?" he asked the others. Paddy nodded. "I remember. They were partners for a short time back in the seventies. A right good team, too. I remember when they cracked the drug case by finding LSD hidden in ice cubes in the freezer of the dealer's house."

Bertie jumped in. "That's right. Tommy was thirsty. It was a hot day and he got himself a glass of ice water from the dealer's kitchen."

"After searching the premises," Bertie interjected.

Sean took over. "The dealer had wrapped LSD tabs in cellophane and stuck them in the individual compartments of the trays. While Tommy was sipping his water, Charlie noticed these funny-looking things floating in the ice. When he realized what it was, he knocked the glass from Tommy's hand before the ice melted completely. Tommy looked at Charlie like he'd gone daft."

Sean turned to me. "But since you're Charlie's niece, you ought to know the scheme they cooked up when it was discovered that our chief of police was cheating at poker."

"Instead of confronting him, which would have cost

him his job, he consulted with Tommy and they switched the card decks," Bertie said as a fresh stout was poured for everyone by Bernie. "Everyone but the chief knew that the new deck was specially marked. The players took turns winning until everyone ended up with the same amount they'd started out with. To this day, I don't think the chief ever discovered the trick pulled on him that night."

"At least he's not using the same method as back then," Paddy added.

After promising to return soon to hear more stories about Tommy, I got up to leave. I had enjoyed listening to the men spin their stories and intended to join them again for more stories about Uncle Charlie. If I hadn't been on a case, I could have stayed there a few more hours and listened to this unofficial wake for Tommy Grady, retired policeman. I think Grady's friends enjoyed having a new ear to bend, as well.

*It's too bad I don't know who was supposed to meet Grady,* I thought. *I'd like to talk to the person who never kept his appointment.*

Then it hit me like a jab to the solar plexus. I felt so stupid. It was possible that the appointment *had* been kept—an hour and a half late! The person Grady had spoken to on the phone might be the murderer.

# ♣ Chapter 10

*I* stepped out onto Washington Street and squinted. It was hard for me to believe that it was still daylight after spending so much time in the smoky and dark Wild Irish Rose. I checked my watch. It was five-thirty. People were rushing up and down the street, leaving work to catch cabs or to walk briskly toward Park Street Station.

Then there were those who lingered in front of the various clubs, eyeing longingly those showcase photos that promised that the potential customer would be assured of gorgeous, slender, tanned, modellike girls who were willing—eager, even—to strip to seductive tunes.

I scanned the area where the body had been found, trying to picture in my mind how it had happened. There were two clubs and three bars nearby, possible places for witnesses to be exiting or entering at the time of the murder. One of the clubs had a side entrance for the "exotic dancers" to slip in and out of, an entrance that was across the street from where Grady was killed. An open parking lot down the block also faced the Dumpster next to the Exchange, a bar for transvestites and transsexuals.

I crossed the street in the middle of the block and entered the Goode Times Club. Inside, I waited for my eyes to adjust to the murky atmosphere, then I went to the bar and ordered a five-dollar beer. When the bartender brought it to me, I casually asked, "So is it true there was a murder down here a few days ago?"

I didn't get an enthusiastic reception at the Goode Times. This bartender gave me one of the weariest now-I've-heard-it-all looks I've ever seen. "Which one?" he asked flatly. "There's at least one murder a night in the Zone."

Yeah, I felt foolish, but then, I was getting paid pretty well. Besides, I had learned during my time as a military investigator that I could sometimes get people to talk if I acted dense. They felt obligated to explain something to you and nine times out of ten, they would inadvertently let something vital slip out.

So I said, "Oh, I mean the ex-cop. I sorta knew him." I got the feeling that this was not the time to whip out my private investigator's license.

The bartender shifted from one foot to the other and replied, "Yeah, I guess so. What's your interest?"

I took a sip of barely cold beer and said, "Like I said, I knew him."

The barkeep narrowed his eyes suspiciously and asked, "You a cop? Why are you nosin' around here?"

While his grammar wasn't impeccable, I got the drift. So I backed off a bit, shrugged, and said, "Just curious. I met him a couple of times."

The barkeep fell silent and withdrew, keeping an eye on me. He continued to polish a beer glass for all it was worth—which wasn't much, but I'm sure that was the best polishing job the guy had ever done on a glass.

I smelled the faint aroma of stale vomit as I glanced around the room. The floor was probably mopped with just water, no ammonia to take the smell away. It was a spacious room with little round tables crammed together as tightly as possible so management could get the largest number of people in here. I was pretty sure that management ignored the fire safety limit sign on the wall that stated only a 250-person capacity. There was little in the way of decoration, but it tended to run toward Early Apathy. There were a few halfhearted attempts on the walls—a half-painted wall in back, a start at red-flocked wallpaper on another side. The floor was chipped tile, probably there since the 1960s. I didn't know what the original color of the tiles had been, but over the years it had turned black with accumulated grime.

The stage had a runway with the now requisite fire pole at the end of it for the dancers to leap on and slither down in the most suggestive manner possible. At the moment, a woman was up there in high heels and some sort of white thing that looked like a diaper. She was listlessly dancing to an old song by Barbra Streisand called "My Heart Belongs to Me." She stopped dancing and lay down on the stage, her legs bent, and lifted her body in time to the words "my heart be-looongs to me . . ." arching her back up on the high note, then letting herself down flat on the floor the last two notes. If she hadn't looked so pathetic, it might have been humorous.

I have no quarrel with those who make stripping their living, but I've always thought it was a pretty sad career choice. If it was a choice, that is. I think it could be safely assumed that there were a number of women whose pick of careers came down to stripping or McDonald's—and stripping pays better.

The Goode Times was starting to fill up with those men who had just gotten off work and who were ready to relax. Maybe it was the loosened ties and rolled-up sleeves that gave them away, but I decided that most of the nine-to-fivers would be least likely to have been here between ten and midnight on a Friday night. Most of those hardworking folks would either have a date—the Goode Times was probably not on the approved list of places to take a girl—or they would have stayed at home with the wife and kids. Or they were out bowling with the league.

There were a few men scattered around the room who looked like regulars at the club. I took my beer and approached the closest one, a man in his middle forties dressed in a starched white long-sleeved shirt and razor-creased black slacks. His thinning hair was combed back with something slick like Brylcreem—a fashion statement if I ever saw one. It screamed Mormon to me, but I didn't see a stack of Books of Mormon anywhere near him. Maybe he was taking the day off.

I put on my best smile and sat down at his corner table. Every table was equipped with a little fake candle. His light was out. I wasn't sure if this was an indication of the man or if it was just sloppy management.

"Hi," I began brightly. "I saw you sitting here alone and thought you might like some company." I sat down uninvited. "You come here often?" Always start out a conversation with something witty and inoffensive.

He stared at me, looking up and down my body as if he were trying to imagine me without clothes on. I started tapping my fingernails nervously on the tabletop.

Finally he said, "I don't believe I've seen you here before."

My system needed time to digest the fact that this ascetic-looking individual sitting across from me had an Oxford-educated accent. But I couldn't afford to take that time, so I forged ahead with what little wits I had left. "No, this is my first time here."

"Are you a new dancer?" The glint in his eye made me feel like there was something creepy crawling up my back. *Great, a Ph.D. with a gutter mind,* I thought.

I ignored his look and answered, "No, actually I just came in here for a beer. Then I remembered that this club was near the place where an ex-cop was killed last week."

He leaned forward in a conspiratorial manner and said, "You think there was something funny about that murder, too? I've wondered about that ever since I saw it happen."

This was too good to be true. Finding a witness so soon? Well, maybe this wasn't going to turn out to be such a bad interview after all.

"So you witnessed the murder, huh?" I kept it casual. I wasn't about to jump on the guy just because he was a witness to a killing and hadn't done anything about it. He probably had his reasons. He could be hiding from the law, or he might have once been beaten up by a bad cop. I continued, "Can you describe what happened?"

"Sh-sh-sh!" He put his finger to his lips and whispered, "They might be listening to us."

"Who?" I whispered back.

"Them." He indicated the stage. I wondered if he thought there were microphones hidden in the club.

Oookay. I felt I might as well go on, although I could almost hear my hopes come to a screeching halt. "Can you tell me what time you witnessed the murder?"

He stared at me, knitting his brow. "I saw the whole thing last night. In one of my visions."

I took a deep breath. How was I going to get out of this one? I decided to humor him. I put on my best serious face and asked, "Why didn't you go to the police with this information?" There goes my credibility with Detective Randolph.

He said, "I can't do that. The dancers would destroy the earth."

"The dancers?" I asked flatly.

"They communicate with their planet through the

movements they make onstage." He looked around, his expression feverish, before continuing, "I've spent months sitting here, trying to learn their language so I can go to the Air Force's UFO Division with this knowledge. They can stop these alien strippers." Alien strippers? It was beginning to sound like a Russ Meyer movie.

It was all just a little too much for me. He caught my incredulous look and pointed an accusatory finger at me.

"You!" he yelled, his face twisted in madness and rage. "You're in league with them. You may be their leader!"

I got up slowly and started edging away. The other customers stopped what they were doing—drinking and ogling the dancers—to stare in our direction. I thought it would be best to pretend that I hadn't been talking to this lunatic at all. I pulled my chair up to a nearby empty table and tried to look innocent and surprised by this man's crazy behavior. My chances of questioning anyone else in this establishment were getting slimmer by the moment.

It almost worked, but soon I felt a tap on my shoulder. I turned around and stared at a belt buckle. Craning my neck upward, I realized that I was staring up at a giant, better known as a bouncer.

"Joey don't want you here no more," he said gruffly. "You're scarin' away the customers."

I looked around. No one was hightailing it through the front doors, but I decided it probably wasn't in my best interests to point this out. The creature confronting me might not be able to understand my logic. I was also tempted to mention that maybe I wasn't the problem. Maybe the problem was the screwball sitting at the next table, muttering to himself. But again, I kept my thoughts to myself.

Instead, I drained my beer and stood up. I still only came up to the bouncer's chest.

"Take me to your leader," I shouted. It seemed to be the most appropriate response.

he bouncer looked perplexed until I explained why I was there. He nodded and told me to follow him. We went up a set of stairs to the left of the stage and into an office. Joey Goode, owner of the Goode Times Club, resembled a weasel in a bad suit. The suit was a shiny dark blue pinstripe. He wore a tan shirt with it and a forest-green tie. I was tempted to call in Mr. Blackwell or, at the very least, a color consultant.

Goode was dwarfed by his office furnishings; he seemed more like a little kid sitting in his father's chair than the slimy owner of a stripper club in the Zone. His impassive face and assured manner, along with the giant diamond pinky ring and matching tie stickpin, made me suspect that this was a fashion accident with mob connections. I could almost hear *The Godfather* theme music playing softly in the background. When he opened his mouth to speak, I expected to hear some version of Marlon Brando with cotton balls in his cheeks. Instead, I heard a thick, grating Jersey accent.

"This the girl makin' all that trouble downstairs, Frankie?" the weasel asked the behemoth.

Joey? Frankie? Was I in some bad underworld crime

movie from the 1950s? Are all guys named Joey and Frankie destined to work in stripper clubs and run vice? Why not guys named Jason and Frederick?

"Yeah, boss. This's her," Frankie said, then added, "She was talkin' to that guy who comes in here every day. You know, the one who thinks the strippers are aliens who want to take over the world or something."

I smirked. "He thinks they want to destroy earth."

Joey studied me. I shifted from foot to foot, wondering when they'd drag out the cement shoes to punish me for talking to a customer.

Finally he spoke to me. "You make a habit of going around upsettin' customers at clubs? You some kind of women's libber?"

Women's libber? Could he have used a more dated phrase? I had to keep from rolling my eyes. And what is it with these guys—couldn't they pose full questions?

I didn't know whether I was in real trouble with this Joey character or whether this was just an act. Since I couldn't come up with a good lie under these circumstances, I thought it would be best to be honest. I'd already blown it down in the barroom by not being truthful.

"I'm a private investigator," I said, leaning toward him across his desk. "The daughter of the ex-cop who was mugged and killed a few weeks ago hired me to ask around, maybe find a witness."

Joey Goode stared at me, silent. Then he opened a drawer to his right. *This is it,* I thought. *He's going for a gun. I'm dead.* Instead, he pulled out a bottle of brandy and two glasses. I breathed a sigh of relief.

"Drink?" He opened up the bottle.

I didn't think it would be polite to refuse. I nodded. When the brandy was poured, Joey motioned to his trained ape. Frankie reached one massive arm over my shoulder, grabbed my brandy glass in a ham fist, and handed it to me. Then he retreated into the corner to impersonate a giant coat rack until Joey needed his help again.

We sipped our brandy in silence. I decided it would be better to let him talk first.

"So you're a private eye," Joey said, looking me up and down. "If you don't mind my saying so, I think you're much too pretty to be in such a lousy profession."

I shrugged. "It's all I'm qualified to do."

"You got any I.D.? Not that I don't trust you . . ."

I nodded and opened my purse slowly. Joey motioned silently to Frankie, who came over and searched through my belongings until he found my wallet. It was probably just as well that I hadn't brought my gun along. Frankie might have twisted it into a big mass of useless steel if he'd found it.

He handed the wallet to me and I opened it up and took out a business card and my driver's license. Private investigators in Massachusetts didn't get any kind of PI I.D. to carry around—they only get an eight-and-a-half-by-eleven certificate to frame or shove in their file cabinets. Joey Goode squinted at both I.D.s for about half a minute, then said, "Angela Matelli. That sure looks like you." Leaning back in his chair again, he added, "But I can't believe that's all you're qualified to do. I might be able to line something up for you, if you ever want to give up the gumshoe gig."

*Yeah,* I thought, *like prancing around on a stage in a G-string and some sparkle dust. No, thanks.* "Well, I'll think about it," I said in a noncommittal tone. "If I ever get restless enough to change professions, I'll give you a call."

He seemed satisfied with my response. "So what exactly do you want to know about this murder, Angie?" It appeared to be a rhetorical question. He went on, "You just need to ask some people some questions. Find out if anyone witnessed something before or after, right?"

He certainly was able to pin down what I wanted to know. All I could do was nod and wonder how I had all of a sudden become "Angie" to him.

He pulled out a notebook and asked, "What night did this happen?"

I gave him the date. He consulted his notebook before telling me, "Dixie, Bunny, and Ginger were working that night. So was Frankie. You already talked to the bartender downstairs. He was on that night. Of course, none of the girls left at one—their shift ends at two. But sometimes when they have a break, they'll slip out the side entrance to get some air and have a smoke."

Dixie, Bunny, and Ginger. I wondered if there was a Bambi as well. I asked, "So are you saying that you're going to let me interview your employees?"

"Of course. Why not? The cops didn't come in and ask any questions after the body was found." He raised his hands in an expansive gesture. "But, Angie, we have nothing to hide. Of course, only Bunny is here right now. But by the time you're finished talking to her, Dixie and Ginger should be coming in for their shift."

Joey Goode pulled a cigar out of a box on the desk, cut the end off, and stuck it in his mouth. Without any prompting, Frankie was by his side with a lighter. After a few puffs, Joey said, "So why don't I leave you in Frankie's hands, so to speak. He'll take you down to the dressing room and explain things to Bunny."

I rose and replied, "Thanks for your help."

Joey shrugged. "I don't know what good it's gonna do you. I don't think you're gonna get much info out of those broads. They're all missin' a tassel up here"—he grinned, tapped his temple with his cigar hand, and added—"if you know what I mean."

"Well, this is way more than I expected."

Joey Goode laughed and replied, "Bet you thought we were a buncha mob-connected hoods, right?"

I forced a laugh and started to leave. Joey had one more thing to say, though. "Say, Angie." I turned around. "I really mean it about that job offer. I bet you'd look great in some of those costumes." He made an hour-glass with his hands. "Vavoom! And I bet you can dance, too. We have amateur night every Wednesday at eight. Stop by anytime."

I was led downstairs to the dressing room, a badly lit unpainted brick room with several broken-down tables with lighted mirrors attached. Cheap eyeshadow, glitter, and false eyelashes were scattered around the vanity surfaces. Frankie nodded to me and started to back out.

I stopped him. "Joey said you were here that night. Did you happen to step out of the club between one and one-fifteen?"

Frankie grunted and replied, "Nah. I stay in the club till the very end. What kind of bodyguard would I be if I stepped outside for a moment and some crazy comes in with an AK-47 to shoot up my boss?"

I had to satisfy my curiosity. "Tell me, Frankie, why does Joey need a bodyguard?"

Frankie looked at me like I was insane and replied, "If you were the owner of a strip club, wouldn't you hire protection?"

I was beginning to see. "So he needs you to protect him from other greedy businessmen."

"What businessmen? I protect him from all those loony antiporn groups. He's always getting threatening phone calls and letters. Once someone actually wired a bomb under his car, but it didn't work right." He looked at his watch and said, "Bunny should be finishing her act by now. I'll send her in." He slipped out the door, leaving me to mull over my foolish assumption that the mob was after Joey's business. That was in the good old days, I guess. Life was so much simpler before all those anti-this and anti-that groups came along.

A few minutes later, a very sweaty blonde came into the room, wearing nothing but a G-string and a short green polyester robe. She had a towel thrown around her neck and looked weary from all the gyrating she must have done onstage.

She looked at me with friendly curiosity. "You must be the private eye Frankie told me about."

"You must be Bunny," I replied. "My name's Angela."

She smiled and said, "Linnea, when I'm not working." Bunny, now Linnea to me, sat down at one of the less rickety vanities and peered into the mirror. She made a face. "Geez. I don't think I'll be doing this too much longer. I got wrinkles galore." She started spreading cold cream on her face, rubbing it in vigorously.

From where I sat, she looked fine. Linnea added, "Of course, that's what face-lifts are for." She turned to me and said, "So you're looking into the death of an ex-cop from a few days ago?"

"Yes. It was Friday night."

Linnea cocked her head to the side and said, "I remember hearing about it the next day. I saw a report of it on television. Wow, I thought, someone was killed just outside the club at the same time that I was working. That's some coincidence."

"Yeah," I agreed, "some coincidence. Did you happen to take a break at one or anytime after? Maybe you stepped outside the side entrance for a breath of fresh air."

She laughed. "The air may not be all that fresh in here, but it ain't so great out there, either. Car exhaust, the stench of vomit, guys gettin' their kicks from hasslin' me." She shook her head. "I just stay inside now till the end of my shift. Then I go home to my kid."

*The wild life of a stripper,* I thought.

"Do you know if any of the other dancers might have been out there on that night?" I asked.

She took a cigarette from a purse near the vanity. After she lit it, blue smoke curling up toward the ceiling, she said, "I think Dixie might have taken a break, but I don't know what time. She sometimes goes out there to—" Bunny/Linnea made a snorting sound. I got the picture. "She scores from someone who hangs around all the bars on this street."

I thanked her just as two other women came tripping into the dressing room.

"Hey, Linnea!" said a tall woman with creamy coffee skin and reddish brown hair. She wore a big grin. "Are you decent?"

Linnea made a snickering sound and replied, "Are you kidding? Never!" She indicated me to the women and introduced me. "Ginger, Dixie, this is the private eye Joey wants you to talk to. Her name's Angela."

Ginger turned out to be the woman who addressed Linnea as she walked in. Dixie was a little dark-haired girl who might be mistaken for jailbait if you didn't get too close to look at the deep lines around her eyes.

Dixie talked to me first. I could tell she was wired and probably wanted to get her interview over with so she could get high again before her first performance. I figured it out when I saw her arms had the scabbed and bruised tracks of a junkie.

"So what do you want to know?" Dixie asked. Her tone was already very defensive. She sat on a chair facing me, defiant from the start. I got the impression that she was not a happy person.

When you do this kind of work for as long as I have—even in the military—you get so you can read people. Dixie had a chip on her shoulder a mile wide. Her head was cocked back as if she were waiting to pounce on me for some imagined slight to her character, one of her legs was beating an impatient tattoo, and she crossed her arms tightly in front of her body.

I got the impression that she didn't have much of a sense of humor. This was a woman who had had the life sucked out of her at one point, whether by coke, horse, or just a lousy childhood, I didn't know. Probably a combination of all three.

Dixie would have to be handled with kid gloves. I explained as gently as I could. "I'm trying to find out if anyone might have stepped out on their break the night of the murder. Maybe you saw something that would give me a clue."

Her head twitched back slightly. "So you're wondering if I was outside the club about the time this guy was whacked."

I nodded.

"Well, I wasn't," she said defiantly.

Ginger interrupted. "What do you mean, girl? I saw you step out that door about one. You were going to meet your connection."

Dixie's anger turned away from me and focused on Ginger. "Why don't you just shut up, bitch! What do you know! You were screwing Frankie in the back room while Bunny was onstage."

Ginger narrowed her eyes, her jaw set. The tension was so thick I would have had trouble cutting it with a chainsaw. I was beginning to wonder if I'd have to break up a cat fight. But Ginger smiled coolly, crossed her arms casually, and said, "What would you know about it, Dixie? You have such a dirty mind. Just because two people enjoy each other's company don't mean they're screwing each other every chance they get."

Dixie snarled, then turned back to me. "I didn't see nothin', didn't hear nothin', don't know nothin'." I could see she was starting to get the shakes. Had to be heroin. Crack's bad, but heroin withdrawal's worse.

I tried again. "Look, Dixie. I'm not here to pass judgment on how you live your life. But if you could give me the name of your connection, maybe he saw something—"

She stood up abruptly and said, "Interview's over, lady. Go fuck yourself. I ain't talkin' to you no more." Dixie stomped out the door, taking care to bring her purse, which probably had her rig in it.

I turned to Ginger and Linnea. Both were shaking their heads at Dixie's exit. Linnea looked disgusted, but there was stark pity in Ginger's eyes. "That girl's the walking wounded if I ever saw it," she said. I was beginning to like Ginger quite a bit.

Linnea added dryly, "Horse can do that to you."

Ginger sighed and looked at me. "I don't think I can help you much. As Dixie so tactfully suggested, Frankie and I were screwing in the storeroom."

I raised my eyebrows and said, "But you just told her—"

Ginger laughed, Linnea chuckled. "Yeah, well," Ginger replied, "I don't like to let her know she's right some of the time."

I grinned and stood up. "Well, I appreciate the time you've taken to talk to me. By the way, does someone named Bambi work here?"

Linnea stubbed out her cigarette and said, "Yeah, Bambi works here. You know her?"

I'd thought so. Every stripper club had to have a Bambi. I smiled at my private joke, shook my head, and said, "Not really."

Ginger came up to me and touched my elbow. "For what it's worth, Dixie's connection is someone named Eileen. I've only seen her a few times, and it's always been in that dark alley. But she's about six feet tall, straight blond shoulder-length hair that's too perfect. It just has to be a wig. And she has brown eyes and a mole on the left side of her cheekbone. I don't think that's real, either."

"How can I find her?" I asked.

Linnea spoke up. "When she's not working the bars, she hangs out at the Exchange."

I nodded, then did a double-take. "The Exchange. Isn't that—"

Ginger and Linnea broke into whoops of laughter. I thanked them again and as I left, I heard Ginger say, "You got your work cut out for you, girl!"

It was going to be a long night.

## ♣ Chapter 12

When I left the Goode Times, it was dark and my stomach was growling. I realized I hadn't eaten anything since breakfast. My watch told me it was only six-thirty. Although I'm not privy to the habits of drug connections, I thought it was safe to assume that Eileen wouldn't start her circuit until after eight o'clock. Plenty of time for me to go to the Golden Gate, a little restaurant in Chinatown only a few blocks away from the Exchange.

I hoofed it over there and was surprised to be seated immediately. Usually the Gate is crammed wall-to-wall with people. I ordered my usual, beef with broccoli, and polished off everything on my plate. I topped it off with one of their egg custard tarts. The tarts are hard to describe, but once you taste one, you wish you could have one every day for the rest of your life.

I went back to the Zone to work the streets, trying to turn up Eileen, the drug-pushing transvestite. Do you ever stop and wonder if you're in some kind of surreal sitcom, but you just don't know it? That's how I felt when I entered the Exchange; it was like entering another world. The customers looked like women, talked like women, and acted like women, but there was something a little left of center about the whole scene. Maybe it was the fact that they looked, talked, and acted a little too much like women, or their idea of what a woman should be.

I should have fit right in, except that I felt a little underdressed for the occasion in my jeans. Most of the customers wore cocktail dresses. Several groups of transvestites were eyeing me, so I walked over to the bar and ordered a beer.

One of Sade's latest tunes was playing on the jukebox. The bartender wore a stunning black leather dress with a rhinestone-studded neckline. His red wig had been teased in a sort of modified Ann-Margret style. His makeup was a tasteful combination of peach and mauve. If it weren't for the five o'clock shadow peeking through his peaches 'n' cream blusher, I'd say he had a pretty good chance of passing as a woman.

When he came back with my beer, I slid a ten spot across to him and asked, "Is Eileen here yet?"

He hesitated.

"It's important," I said, adding another ten spot to the one I was already offering. He nodded and pointed across the room to a tall blond woman standing near the jukebox.

As I approached Eileen, I noticed that the jukebox was near the restrooms. A convenient location for the up-and-coming drug dealer—slip into a stall with a client, make the exchange away from prying eyes, then back out near the jukebox in search of the next sucker.

I was surprised at how feminine Eileen appeared. There was no stubble and no hard masculine lines to the face, something that most often gave away a cross-dresser. The blond hair appeared to be real, not a wig, and fell artfully around the face in soft curls. The makeup job was better than anything I could slap on before I went out on a date. Eileen's ensemble was less flamboyant than the bartender's, but more businesslike. The two-piece blue miniskirt and black blazer hugged the body, which had more curves than I would ever see. She—I was already starting to think of him as a her—carried a black satin evening purse. I wondered if that was where she kept her wares.

"Hi." I smiled. "Looks like you need a new drink. Can I buy you one?"

Eileen looked momentarily disconcerted. She glanced around the room as if she weren't certain that she was in the right bar. Then she looked back at me, a mixture of wariness and curiosity on her face. The curiosity won out.

"Sure," she replied. "Bourbon and water."

I grabbed a passing "waitress" and gave her the order, adding another beer to the tab. Then I spied an empty table and gestured to Eileen.

Instead she led me to a corner table, greeting her friends and acquaintances along the way. They all looked at me with the same curiosity as Eileen had a few moments ago. In this place, I felt like a freak. Now I knew how they must feel in the outside world.

We sat. I studied her, looking for the details that gave away the fact that Eileen was male. It wasn't easy to imagine the man underneath the layers of makeup, dress, and permed hair, but I think I got a fair idea of what the real Eileen looked like. As a man, she would be tall and slender with sleek muscular arms. The chin was strong with a thin mouth and a Roman nose above it. The eyes were a little too close set, but they were a warm brown.

"So is this a pickup?" she asked coyly. Her voice was husky like Lauren Bacall's. Any man who met her and didn't know that she was a he would want to take her home immediately.

I fought a smile. "I wish it were. But I'm a private investigator. Angela Matelli."

She sighed and replied, "I suppose you know my name already."

"Well, I know your name is Eileen around here."

"Look," she said seriously, "maybe I don't want to talk to you."

"But you don't even know what I've come here to see you about. Aren't you the least bit curious?"

Our drinks came and I paid. Eileen hesitated, bit her lip, then nodded.

I asked, "You know a dancer named Dixie?"

"Maybe," she answered cautiously. "Why do you want to know? Did she get busted again?"

I shook my head. "Sorry. Let me explain."

Eileen sipped her bourbon and water and listened to my explanation. When I was finished, she had a look of relief on her face.

"So all you want to know is if I was in the alley that night and if I saw anything."

"Yeah," I said. "I've been hired to find the killer, so I'm looking for anyone who might have been in view of the Dumpster next to this bar. That's where Tom Grady's body was found." I leaned slightly forward and asked, "So can you help me? None of this is official. I'm just interested in getting a lead on this murder."

The wary look disappeared and Eileen nodded. Her features twisted in thought. She closed her eyes and murmured, "Last Friday." A few moments later, she opened her eyes. "Yeah, I met Dixie a little after one. She needed a fix bad. She had the shakes when I got there. We did our business, then she got her rig out and shot up right there. I stood lookout."

Eileen stopped, seeing the disgust on my face. She had the grace to look down at her drink, embarrassed.

I took a moment to get my feelings under control, then said, "Sorry about that. I really have no right to judge. Just, sometimes . . ." I changed the subject. "Why?"

She looked up, surprised. "What do you mean?"

"I mean, why? Why sell the stuff, knowing it hurts people?" The minute I said it, I regretted it. I knew I'd have trouble getting her to open up now.

Her eyes narrowed, her face displayed anger, and she started to stand up. I grabbed her wrist. "Sit down," I said sternly. In a gentler tone, I added, "Please."

She continued to stare at me, but she didn't try to break away. Finally Eileen sat down slowly and said, "I don't have to take that from you. I don't have to answer your questions. Just go away and leave me alone."

I sighed and ran my hand through my hair. Boy, I screwed up on this one. "Look, I apologize. It was unfair. I don't know you, but I guess the drug thing, I'll never understand."

She drained her bourbon and water. I signaled a passing waitress for another round. I drank half my beer.

"Look," I said, "we just won't talk about it. It was totally unprofessional of me to even bring it up. I should get used to this."

"How long have you been a private eye?" she asked.

"I just started my own agency a few weeks ago," I confessed. "I was a military investigator before that."

Eileen nodded. I was feeling slightly humiliated that I was unburdening my personal work history on this transvestite. I knew that this wasn't the way to conduct an investigation. I'd blown it for the second time today. Maybe my problem was that in the military, I didn't have to go through some of the preliminary exchanges between investigator and potential witness that go on in civilian life.

"I guess that explains your abrupt manner," she said.

Back in the Marines, when I had to interrogate someone, the person in question was brought to my office and I conducted the interview without beating around the bush. The Marine knew what was expected of him or her and usually would answer without hesitation. We didn't talk about the weather and we didn't discuss the reason for the interviewee being there, unless I decided to bring it up. Now I was in the real world and had to play by a different set of rules. And I was learning the hard way, by making mistakes.

I sighed, suddenly feeling very weary. It had been a very long day. I just wanted to go home and relax in a hot bath. Maybe I'd even use some of that fragrant herbal bath oil that Rosa gave me as part of her thank-you for letting her have an apartment at a reduced rent.

Eileen cleared her throat. Our fresh drinks had arrived and, again, I paid for them. I seemed to be drinking a lot today. That might be adding to my exhaustion. I resolved not to have any more. I usually didn't have more than a glass of beer or wine, if I drank at all.

I turned my attention back to Eileen. "So, can we start over? I'll stay out of your business if you can answer my question."

She nodded. "I know what I do is pretty slimy—"

I held up a hand to stop her, but she shook her head and said, "No, I want to tell you now. I don't like what I do, either, but I'm taking hormones, getting ready for an operation. And it's expensive. I was let go from my job when it became apparent that I was in the middle of a sex change." She opened her little purse, took out a cigarette, and lit it. "I was in a high-profile job, so I guess I can't blame them too much. So with no money, no insurance, which probably wouldn't have paid for my operation anyway, and now no job, I started selling. First it was to just a few friends, then my reputation grew. So here I am in the Zone."

I tried to look appropriately sympathetic. She sipped her drink, then said, "Once I'm a woman, I plan to quit selling and get another job in my old profession, if the job market gets better."

"What did you do before this?"

"Director of an art gallery on Newbury Street."

I raised my eyebrows. Everyone in Boston knew that the Newbury Street condos and apartment buildings were almost exclusively gay. Eileen must have known what I was thinking because she added, "I know. Newbury Street has mostly gays and yuppies living there. But the business owners aren't necessarily more open-minded than any other area."

I had to concede that she had a point. I was just starting to wonder how to bring the conversation back to the murder when she said, "Let's talk about what you came here for."

I was relieved. Listening to a transvestite's confession of the woes that befell his/her quest for a sex change operation didn't exactly fall into the category of subjects I would most like to talk about. Not that I had anything against transvestites, transsexuals, gay men, or lesbians, for that matter. Despite the regulation that a gay man or woman cannot enlist, I'm sure I knew plenty of them in the armed forces. They just weren't openly gay, and it wouldn't have been wise for them to open up to others. If I had discovered that a friend of mine had a sexual preference different from my own, I wouldn't have felt right about reporting it to my higher-ups. It was none of my business. It was none of the military's business. I have always thought that gays were just like anyone else: There were some I liked and some I didn't like, and none of it had anything to do with their sexual orientation.

I focused my attention back on Eileen. She was tracing patterns on the wet tabletop while she was talking. "We left off at the point where I was playing lookout for Dixie while she was shooting up. When she was done, she went back inside and I stepped out of the alley, ready to go back across the street to this place." She closed her eyes again as if she were trying to picture the scene in her mind. "I ran into another customer and we stepped back just inside the alley to make a transaction. While I was waiting, I watched the street for cops."

I nodded encouragingly, deciding against saying anything to disturb her concentration. "I saw . . ." she faltered, opened her eyes and let out a deep breath, then shook her head. "I don't think I saw anything."

"Can I ask you some questions? It might jog your memory."

She nodded.

"How busy was the street?"

"There were a few people on Washington. Around one, most of the serious perverts and alcoholics are busy bending their elbows at one of the clubs or pubs. There were a few street people wandering around looking for a handout, and some couples who were trying to be casual about slipping into a club or the adult store down the street that sells sex toys."

I asked another question. "Did anyone come out of any of the places across the street, anyone who might have looked like a regular from one of the bars?"

She stared into space. I wanted to scream "The Wild Irish Rose!" at her, but I didn't want ask a leading question, and that would qualify. Finally, she snapped her fingers.

"The Rose. A guy came out of the Rose." Without

prompting, she described him. "I think he was about your height, maybe a little taller. I'm terrible with heights, especially at a distance. But he had white hair, probably was in his early sixties, but looked to be in good health. Maybe a little stocky."

I let out the breath I'd been holding and asked, "What did he do?"

"He walked past the parking lot, which I suppose means he didn't drive there. That's the direction you'd go to get to the Essex T Station."

"Then what happened?" I asked eagerly. Too eagerly.

Her answer deflated my zeal. "Nothing," she said. "That was it. My customer left and I came back here." Eileen finished her bourbon and cocked her head to the side. "Was that what you were looking for?"

I covered my disappointment with a grateful smile. "If I showed you a picture of the murder victim, do you think you could identify it?"

She shrugged. I pulled three pictures out of my wallet. One was the picture of Tom Grady that Sheilah had given me, and the other two were of my uncles, Sharkey and "No-Legs" Charlie (pictured above the waist, of course). All three were white-haired men in their sixties.

Eileen studied each one briefly, then pointed to Tom Grady. I felt a sense of relief. Unfortunately, it was followed by the feeling that I really hadn't gotten anything important, other than the fact that Tom Grady had definitely been at the Wild Irish Rose that night (which had been confirmed by his cronies already), and that he'd walked in the direction of Essex Station, which meant that he walked past the Dumpster where his body was found.

"Is that all?" she asked, looking at her watch. "I have an appointment in a few minutes."

I was about to say good-bye, but something made me

ask, "Eileen, did you see anyone leave the pub after Grady, or anyone on the street near the Rose who might have been following him? Someone who could have stopped him?"

"Man or woman?"

I shrugged and watched her closely. Then she nodded. "There was a couple walking toward him. Then there was this fellow who was leaning against a building near the Rose. As I recall, he left, walking behind the murder victim. But at the time, I just thought he was leaving because he'd either been stood up or he hadn't found anything he liked."

"What did he look like?" I asked.

She furrowed her brow, then shook her head. "That's a hard one. I don't memorize faces. I might be able to pick out someone who looked like him if I was shown a photo, but . . ." she trailed off, still frowning.

"But you were able to give me a description of Grady. You even picked him out of these photos," I pointed out.

She smiled and said, "But I was watching out for cops, and this guy looked like a cop." Eileen paused, waiting for confirmation.

"He was a cop," I said. "How did you know that?"

She looked satisfied, explaining, "Most of us on the wrong side of the law tend to have a sixth sense about cops, even when they're plainclothes. Of course, it doesn't always work, but I've been pretty lucky. I've developed my powers of observation in order to survive. For instance, I knew you had to have some military training because of the way you walk. Cops have a way of walking and a certain air of authority."

"But Tom Grady was retired," I pointed out.

She laughed. "Even retired cops have it. Once you have it, it's hard to get rid of. Sort of like the feelings I have that I'm a woman trapped in a man's body."

"If you're so observant, how come when I first came up to you, you thought I was trying to pick you up?"

Eileen looked around the bar coyly. "You do know where you are, don't you?"

I followed her gaze, then nodded. I felt so sheltered suddenly. She said, "We get women in here who want something different. They come in all shapes and sizes. I don't judge 'em, just as I hope they don't judge me." She looked at her watch again. "Darlin', I've got to go."

As she stood up to leave, I asked, "If I came around again in the next week with some pictures, is it possible that you could pick out the man who was walking toward Tom Grady?"

Eileen shrugged. "I might be able to."

"Was he old or young?"

"He looked like he was in his late thirties, early forties."

"Height?"

She shrugged. "From almost one hundred yards, it was hard to tell. Taller than the victim."

"Race?"

"White male, brown hair." She snapped her fingers and said, "I don't know if this will help any, but he either had a beard or a very long jaw. If it was a beard, it was closely trimmed. It was night and some of the streetlights on that side of the street are burned out. I really gotta go."

I stood up and shook hands. "I really appreciate the information."

"No problem. You can find me here most nights around this time. Thanks for the drinks."

With that, she was gone.

## ♣ Chapter 13

It was almost ten o'clock when I got home and dragged myself up the stairs. As I climbed up to the second-floor landing, I wondered if Rosa was home. I hadn't seen or spoken to my little sister since Sunday morning. The lights were on and there was music playing, so I stopped and rapped on the door. Someone turned down the music inside, but Rosa still didn't come to the door.

I knocked again. There was still no answer. I considered calling her name or using my key to get inside. Maybe she was hurt or, worse, some crazed rapist or killer was inside. I shook my head. *You're losing it, Sarge,* I thought, using Rosa's affectionate term. Too much violence in my life lately must have shaken loose what few bolts I have left.

So I stomped up the stairs and spent a restless hour rattling around in my spartan apartment. After fixing myself a snack of hazelnut and chocolate spread on Italian bread, I picked up the phone and dialed Rosa's number. I couldn't stop worrying about her. I guess I took over the mother hen role when she moved out of Ma's.

A sleepy male voice answered, deep, warm, and sexy. "Hello?"

I pulled the phone away from my ear and stared into the receiver. *I must have misdialed,* I thought. I hung up and tried again. This time, Rosa answered. "Hello."

"Rosa."

"Sarge! I haven't seen you for days."

"Yeah, I know. I've been as busy as a hooker in the Combat Zone on a Friday night."

Rosa groaned, then said, "I went up and knocked on your door this morning, but you were already gone. When did you get in?"

So Rosa had been worried about me these past few days. I guess I wasn't the only one with mother hen instincts.

"Just a few minutes ago," I replied. "Didn't you hear me knocking?"

There was a pause. She finally said, "There's, uh, someone here right now."

It finally dawned on me—the male voice that had answered the first time. I hit my head with the heel of my hand. "So that wasn't a wrong number. What would Ma think of her little Rosa at a time like this?"

She laughed. "Angie! Actually, that's probably why I didn't answer the door when you knocked. I suddenly had this vision of living in Ma's house and sneaking a boy into my room."

"Well, you're not living with her now," I reminded her. "Please. I'm not Ma. I promise if I meet this guy—"

She supplied his name. "Ron."

"—Ron," I continued, "I won't ask him what his intentions are or what he does for a living."

"Thank you," she said, relief obvious in her voice.

"I already know what his intentions are." We both laughed. I sobered and said, "Speaking of Ma, how was Sunday dinner?"

"She wondered where you were. All through dinner

she kept asking, 'Where's Angela? Tell me again, Rosa, why couldn't she come?' I had to keep telling her that you'd gotten a very important case. I hated lying."

"You didn't lie. I got a case this week. That's why I've been gone so much," I said.

"Yeah, but I told her on Sunday. You didn't get the case till Monday."

Well, technically I didn't get the case until yesterday morning, Wednesday, but I wasn't going to nitpick. "Rosa, Rosa. A day here, a day there. What's the difference? I won't tell Ma if you won't."

"Can you come down here for a drink, maybe meet Ron?"

My head was still buzzing from all the alcohol I'd tossed down in all those bars. "Make it herbal tea and you're on."

Rosa was at the door when I got there. The smell of recently burning candles filled the air. Thank heavens she used the ordinary kind, not those horrible scented kind like bayberry or potpourri. Strictly for hippie wannabees in the early seventies. I remembered having scented candles and sandalwood incense scattered around my room when I was still in high school. Ma had a heart attack every time she entered my room. She was sure I'd burn the house down someday.

The teakettle was merrily whistling on the gas burner in Rosa's art deco kitchen. As she poured my tea, she said over her shoulder, "I got your note. You've probably already polished off those artichokes."

"That's why you're my favorite sister," I replied, giving her cheek a pat.

"And I gave Sophia the key. She should be moving in sometime this week or next."

"Fine and dandy. How's she doing?"

Rosa laughed and said, "Do you know that she tried

to talk me into switching apartments with her?"

"What?"

Rosa turned around at the sharpness in my voice. She chuckled. "Don't worry. I'm not giving up this place. She tried the sympathy routine on me, then tried to get Ma on her side. I had to put up with it through dinner. I almost asked her for her key back."

My hands had become tight fists. There were times I wished I could knock some sense and common decency into my older sister. Rosa noticed my fists as well and said, "Hey, Sarge. It's all right. She didn't get what she wanted. Ray, Albert, and Vinnie were there with their families to take my side." God bless our brothers.

I growled anyway. Rosa handed me my tea and we went into the living room.

"So where's this Ron you were telling me about?" I asked.

A tall, lean, tanned, bare-chested guy in tight blue jeans walked into the room. He had classic features, straight nose, blue eyes, perfect mouth, and sandy blond hair, wet and slicked back from just having taken a shower. I had to remind myself that he was probably Rosa's age and my sister was interested in him. Watching Rosa stand up and put her arms around him made me realize how nonexistent my own social and sex lives were. For a moment, I almost felt sorry for myself. I had to get a social life soon, then maybe I'd have a sex life.

Rosa introduced us. Ron Ellis turned out to be a philosophy major at Boston University, better known as BU to us locals. *Now there's a major with a lot of job opportunities,* I thought. According to Rosa, they'd met at the restaurant where she worked. He was one of the new chefs.

"So Rosa tells me that you're a private eye," Ron the philosopher said. "That must be interesting work."

I shrugged modestly. "It has its moments."

Ron leaned forward, obviously caught up in the fantasy of private detection, and eagerly asked, "Do you have any exciting cases right now?"

I smiled and said, "Well, I'm currently investigating some insurance claims for Leone and Associates down on Chelsea Street."

The light died out in his eyes. I felt like I'd just killed Bambi in front of him instead of discouraging a common romantic notion about private eye work. I talked to them for a few more minutes to be polite, but I could tell by the way his arm went protectively around her waist that they wanted to be alone. I wanted to be alone as well. I was worn out from the long day I'd put in. It was hard for me to believe that Sheilah Grady had been in my office just this morning. It seemed like yesterday's funeral had been a week ago. If the amount of work I would do on the case tomorrow yielded as little information as it did today, I needed my sleep.

I got up and said good night, secretly giving Rosa the thumbs-up on the way out.

Thursday morning came all too early. When I got back up to my apartment last night after leaving Rosa's, I discovered that it was one o'clock in the morning. It must not have been a school night for either of the lovers down there. Of course, when you're younger, you can get by with less sleep than someone like me who was closing in fast on thirty.

I dressed quickly, ate a toasted onion bagel with chive cream cheese, then drove to Dorchester. I had been deliberating over driving versus subway, but decided that since I didn't know exactly where Tom Grady's house was, I'd be better off in the car in case I needed to depart quickly. Besides, I hadn't driven my car in almost a week and it needed the outing.

Parts of Dorchester were sort of an upscale South Boston. Both Southie and Dorchester had large pockets of inhabitants with Irish last names. The area around Dorchester Bay was more residential, more livable, more middle- and upper-middle income than South Boston.

Grady had lived in a small brownstone house on a quiet street called, appropriately enough, Sullivan Drive. The neighboring houses appeared to be quiet, but I parked down the block, just to be on the safe side. As I approached his house, I noticed that there were still remnants of the fluorescent yellow police tape, but most of it had been torn away.

There were two locks on the door, but the key Sheilah had given me fit both locks. The door opened, so apparently the bottom lock was never used. The inside of the residence of a dead person always has a distinctive odor, whether the victim died at home or not. Maybe it was the smell of dark and dust—I noticed the shades were drawn in all the front rooms—or maybe it's just the imagination of anyone who walks into such a place and disturbs the unnatural silence.

Tom Grady had either been very tidy or someone had tidied up after his death. I could imagine Sheilah going through the rooms with a dustcloth and a vacuum, washing the dirty dishes in the sink, straightening out the magazines on the fake Colonial-style walnut coffee table, and finally, as the sun set, sitting down in the darkening front room and crying over the loss of her dad.

The living room was filled with serviceable furniture. There were no antiques here, just an ordinary, comfortably faded flower chintz couch and a nubbly green La-Z-Boy, worn on the arms. Tom Grady must have lived in it, watching his sports programs. The chair sat squarely in front of a large-screen television, a remote control box resting on the arm of the chair. Celtics pennants decorated the walls, framed service awards, medals, and honors from his time on the police force hung above a fake fireplace. There was very little mess here. A Red Sox mug had made a wet ring, then dried, on a walnut end table near the La-Z-Boy, and a large yellow plastic bowl with a few stale pretzels in the bottom of it sat next to it. An out-of-date *TV Guide* lay on the sofa. This had been Tom Grady's life.

I moved around the room, trying to understand him better. On the fireplace mantel, two framed pictures were displayed. One was of a woman in her forties and a teenager. The woman stood just slightly behind the girl, her hands resting comfortably on the teenage girl's shoulders. Both wore the artificial smiles that we all turn on when we're told to smile for the camera. The teen was a younger Sheilah, maybe ten years younger. I assumed the woman was her mother, Grady's wife. Tom Grady's obituary had mentioned that his wife was deceased.

I picked up the other framed picture. It was a more recent photo of Sheilah, this time with Brian. I found it ironic that in this picture, Sheilah stood slightly behind Brian, her hands resting comfortably on his shoulders. On an impulse, I slipped the photo out of its frame and into my purse, reasoning that I might need it later for identification purposes.

I entered Grady's study next. The room was compulsively neat compared to the living room. At least the living room looked like it had been lived in. I knew I couldn't be the first person to rummage through his belongings. An old-fashioned roll-top walnut desk jutted out from one wall, with a manual typewriter sitting on top of a blotter. A cheap replica of a banker's lamp with a green shade hunched over the typewriter, and there were several sheaves of blank paper stacked neatly on the desk beside the blotter.

I spent a good half hour going through his bookshelves and desk drawers, looking for a clue. A clue to what, I didn't know. I came up empty. I went through the room a second time, this time methodically pulling books off the shelves in order and dumping out the desk drawers. During this more determined search, I found a brochure on the ILAP; it had been stuck in the back of the center drawer, caught in a crack.

I gave it a cursory glance. The name of the organization kept popping up so I slipped it into my shoulder bag to read later.

I was thirsty from all the work I'd done, so I got up and went into the kitchen. The refrigerator must have dated back to the 1940s. I opened the door and hunted for something cold with no expiration date on it. I found a can of diet soda. As I was sitting at the kitchen table sipping my soda, I heard the sound of breaking glass coming from the back door right off the kitchen.

I didn't have much time to decide what to do, but it didn't seem very bright to confront an unknown burglar—even if I did know how to take care of myself. So I left the kitchen and went to the front door. Cautiously, I looked outside. There was a brown Econoline van parked in front of the house with a very large man sitting in the driver's seat. I couldn't get a clear view of what he looked like, but decided not to find out the hard way. I was trapped in the house.

The back door opened and the men—by now, I had determined that there was more than one—walked in. I turned around and climbed the stairs, taking care to step lightly, hoping there wasn't a squeaky board to give me away. *If I'd known there would be trouble, I'd have brought my gun along,* I thought. Hindsight is twenty-twenty.

Nearing the top of the stairs, I began to wonder if these men were the garden-variety burglars. I had always thought that common thieves broke into houses during funerals, not a few days after. When I heard voices heading for the front room, I began to realize that I might not get out of here without being discovered. I strained to hear the voices; there was something odd about the accents, but they were so low that I couldn't put my finger on it.

I crept into one of the bedrooms. It had to be Grady's room; a man's robe hung on the back of the door, reading glasses lay on top of a book, and a phone lay on a nightstand next to the bed. *I could dial 911 and have this all taken care of in a matter of minutes,* I thought. With relief, I picked up the receiver. There was no tone. Either the phone company had cut off the service or the burglars had cut the wires, for whatever reason.

I went back to the door and listened. They were still busy downstairs. I looked out the window of the bedroom and noted that part of the back porch roof extended out far enough under the window to reach a large sturdy oak tree.

When I heard their footsteps on the stairs, I ran lightly across the room to the door and locked it. Then I went back, unlocked the window, and tugged at it with all my strength. It wouldn't budge. I pressed against the wooden frame all around, hoping to loosen it enough to get it to open.

The voices were almost outside the door. I struggled, and with a grating squeak of weathered wood and paint, finally succeeded in getting it open.

"Hey! There's someone in there," one of the voices said. The doorknob turned, then a shoulder thudded against the door. I grabbed the book off the nightstand and tossed it out the window, hoping the sound of a book skidding off the roof approximated the sound of a person taking the roof to the tree and escaping. Then I slid under the bed, hidden by a large fringed bedspread.

The door gave way with a loud crack and banged open. A pair of blue and white running shoes and a pair of black motorcycle boots came in. I closed my eyes, praying that they wouldn't start searching the room.

"Damn! The thief got away," said Running Shoes. The accent was unmistakably Irish.

Black Boots laughed. "And what do you think we are, the owners of the house? So what if he got away. We'd better search this room while we're here. Whoever the thief was, he was looking for the same thing. That study was a mess." Black Boots also sounded Gaelic.

"How do you know he didn't find it?" Running Shoes asked.

Black Boots replied, "I don't. But the person who was in this house had a key. There was no sign of forced entry, but he panicked when he heard us enter. So it had to be someone who had permission from the daughter. If we don't find what we're looking for here, we can find out who else had a house key besides Grady's daughter."

They began to search the room. No one looked under the bed, but I had a close call when one of them started to pull up the mattress. I realized that the next thing to be pulled up was the box spring, and then it would be all over for me. I started to edge toward the side nearest the open window.

Suddenly Black Boots hissed, "There's nothing here. We'd better search the other rooms fast. Whoever got away may call the police." A pillowcase was tossed on the floor.

I didn't leave my hiding place when I heard the two burglars going through the rest of the upstairs rooms. I didn't leave when I heard them go down the stairs. I didn't leave when all I heard was quiet in the house. I didn't leave even when I heard the faint roar of a van driving away from the house. I waited almost half an hour, heart pounding the whole time. Only then did I extract myself from under the bed, creep cautiously down the stairs, and leave the house.

I was thankful that I'd driven here and parked my car down the block to avoid suspicion. And I regretted that all I'd seen of the burglars, from under the bed, was their footwear.

I thought about calling Sheilah to notify her about the burglars, but decided that an anonymous call to the Dorchester police would be better. I wasn't sure how I would handle the burglary in my report to Sheilah. I wanted to just skip that part, but I knew I couldn't do that.

Although I knew I had done the right thing, I felt a little sheepish about not confronting the burglars, throwing them over my shoulder to subdue them, and hauling them in to the police.

When I recalled the conversation between the burglars while I was hiding under the bed, it sounded as if they had some connection to Sheilah. I would bet my bottom dollar that the link was Brian Scanlon.

My hands were shaking as I tried to jam the key into the ignition. I was so uncoordinated that it took three times to start the engine.

# ♣ Chapter 14

$I$ drove my car back to East Boston, then took the T to the North End. On the way to work, I stopped at a deli for a roast beef and provolone sandwich and a coffee, then walked briskly to my office. The first thing I noticed when I stepped into the room was that the green light on my answering machine was blinking. Before I checked the messages, I put in an anonymous call to the Dorchester police and told the dispatcher that I'd seen a prowler on the premises of a house in my neighborhood. Then I gave her the Grady residence address and hung up before she could ask for my name and address.

When I finally played back my machine, the first message was from Ma, wondering if I'd make it to the family dinner this coming Sunday. "Even you need to take a day off now and again, Miss Big Shot Detective," she reminded me. I sighed and shook my head. Maybe Ron would go in my place.

The second message was from Detective Lee Randolph, asking if I had turned up anything yet. The last message was from Sheilah, leaving her office number for me to call her before five.

I leaned back in my chair for a few minutes and enjoyed my sandwich. Food seemed to be the only pleasure I got these days. When I wasn't being mugged, investigating the murder of a former client, cursed at by a hooker with a habit, hiding under beds from burglars, or being nagged to death by my mother, I was eating.

When I finished my lunch, I called Randolph back and told him that I didn't have anything yet, which was sort of true. I only had two leads: One was a transsexual pusher who saw Tom Grady leave the Wild Irish Rose that night and who remembered seeing a man walking after Grady on the street, and the other lead was even slimmer—two pairs of shoes.

I skipped returning my mother's call. She'd catch me at home or tomorrow in the office. I called the number for Sheilah's office and was told that she was out for lunch. I left my name. After I hung up, I looked at my watch and realized that I still had half a workday ahead of me. Then I remembered the footwear I'd seen from under the bed and the Irish accents I'd heard. And ILAP kept popping up. Maybe there was a connection.

I decided to spend the rest of the day skulking around the ILAP offices. I looked up their address in the file I'd started on Tom Grady. Apparently ILAP had temporary offices in Harvard Square where Beacon Street and Mass Ave meet.

I pulled open my left bottom desk drawer and took out my new Nikon 35mm with the built-in telescopic lens. I'd have to buy film when I got to Cambridge. I hadn't had much practice with the Nikon since I bought it. I'd only developed one roll of film, but when I opened that packet of developed photos, I'd been pleased to find decent, if occasionally a little out of focus, pictures. This was an easy camera to use. When I was living at home, Ma had one of those impossible-to-use cameras that invariably cut the heads or feet off the subjects.

I left the office and headed for the T. I was looking for feet, specifically black motorcycle boots and blue-and-white running shoes, but a head would certainly help put the footwear into perspective. I reasoned that the ILAP with its Irish contingency was as good a place to start as any.

When I got to Harvard Square, it was bustling. I don't think I've ever been to the Square when it wasn't full of students looking studious, professors looking professorial, street musicians vying for the dollars of passersby, and tourists of every nationality. I used to love coming down here. When I was growing up, Harvard Square was the hub of the college student's universe and the place where half of the Boston population hung out on weekends. Harvard Square was hip, upscale, always on the cutting edge, a microcosm of higher learning—both scholarly and practical. It still was—only now it was the playground of the demi-hip and teen punks who preferred their music loud and obnoxious.

Through all the years that I had lived in Boston, going to Harvard Square was like visiting another planet, for this skinny Italian kid from East Boston. I had thought about attending Harvard just so I could live near the Square. Unfortunately, my dream of attending Harvard University had very little to do with academics. Not that I was any slouch in the learning department; I was a better-than-average student. Okay, I had a 3.5 grade-point average. But I didn't have the right attitude. I was more interested in hands-on experience rather than spending four years or more sitting in stuffy classrooms, learning about inanimate stuff like history and literature. Maybe that's why I ended up attending the University of Massachusetts, and maybe that's why I left it to join the Marines.

I bought a roll of film at a nearby drugstore, knowing

full well that I was paying much more than I would have paid in East Boston. That's another thing about Harvard Square—the cost of living would have eventually killed me. I still had trouble putting the film in the camera, and since I'd just paid more than the film was worth, I made one of the drugstore clerks install it in the camera for me. Then I pocketed the receipt, to enter in my expense book later, and hoofed it to the ILAP offices.

It was in an impressive storefront with a large computer banner announcing INTERNATIONAL LEAGUE FOR THE ADVANCEMENT OF PEACE taped to the window. On the other side of the glass, I could see the ambiguous shapes of people answering phones, stuffing envelopes, and discussing strategies. I crossed the street and focused my camera on the door to the office and pressed the button for the automatic telephoto lens for a closer view. No one would notice me lurking across the street, clicking off pictures of the Square. Even if I was spotted, they would probably think I was a grad student taking art photos for some college photography class. Besides, there were plenty of strange people lurking around Harvard Square, and those who lived or worked there long enough tended to become indifferent to the bizarre after a while.

It was still cold March weather and I was dressed accordingly in high-top running shoes, jeans, a wool sweater, and my ever-present down vest. I drew a pair of fingerless gloves out of my pocket and slid them on. I wore them for just such special occasions as working a camera on surveillance. I'd cut the fingertips off myself. I felt like the essence of Harvard winter fashion itself.

Someone came out of the office, a young woman in jeans, a white T-shirt with the ILAP logo on it, and a leather jacket slung over her shoulder. If I ever decided to go outside like that in this weather, I'd be a private eye Popsicle.

Although I knew this young woman hadn't broken into Tom Grady's house earlier today, I was counting on human nature: Chances were that the burglars wouldn't rush home to change their shoes after breaking and entering the home of a dead man. They probably assumed that they hadn't been seen.

For the next hour, I stood out on the sidewalk, pointed the camera, and pretended to shoot award-winning pictures. Those who came in and out of ILAP were college student material. Finally, the door opened and Seamus McRaney stepped out. At the sight of him, I caught my breath for a moment as if an electric shock had run through my body. He was with two other men, obviously his right- and left-hand men, from the deferential way they flanked him. Both men were close to six feet tall. One was a muscular guy with brown hair and mustache with stubble. He looked to be in his late twenties and wore black motorcycle boots. The other fellow was probably in his early thirties, slender, with light red hair and a neatly trimmed beard. He wore blue and white running shoes.

They paused outside the door as McRaney gestured to make his point about whatever they were discussing. I pointed my camera, hoping I got all of them in the picture, and shot a couple of exposures with the automatic telephoto lens. Then I retracted the lens and shot a couple more, hoping this time the camera was focused.

The trio moved on up Mass Ave toward the hub of the Square. I followed casually, as if I'd decided to go in that direction by chance, at a good distance from them. They stopped at the newsstand on the island in the center of Harvard Square and bought a couple of papers. McRaney continued to lead the conversation, talking animatedly and intensely. He gestured to the paper he was holding. I focused my camera on the newspaper and magnified the lens. I made out the identifying banner above the headlines, which read *The Irish Free Press*.

They moved on; I stayed with them. When they disappeared around the corner of the newsstand, I knew they were taking the T somewhere. I crossed the street, heading for the island, then ran around the corner and descended the stairs to the turnstiles. A train was pulling away as I looked around the nearly empty platform. They must have slipped into one of the cars just before the doors closed.

I stamped my foot in exasperation, but all it got me was a temporary numb feeling that spread up my ankle to my calf. Then I went back to the newsstand and bought a copy of *The Irish Free Press*, the one I'd seen Seamus McRaney buy earlier. The front headlines made my blood run cold: TWELVE KILLED IN EXPLOSION ON ST. STEPHEN'S GREEN.

I read on. It'd been a workday and the buses were on strike that week. The bomb threat had come in to the Office of Transportation that morning, and they had tried to negotiate with the bus drivers to come back to work just for the day, but the drivers refused. People had rushed out of work at five and had started to head for home, using other modes of transportation that ranged from cars to bicycles to foot. When one man tried to start his car, he tripped a bomb that was wired to the ignition. Eleven bystanders were caught in the blast. This had happened not in Northern Ireland, but in Dublin, the capital of the Republic of Ireland. Of course, the IRA had immediately claimed responsibility for it.

I looked at my watch; it was close to five. I hadn't been in the Square for a long time, so I ducked into the Harvard Coop—which is pronounced like the place where chickens go to roost—to do some browsing.

The Coop has become a legend around Boston. The

main store sits on the corner across from the Harvard T station, but when you go through the store to the very back, you can leave by the back door and emerge on a side street. On the other side of the street, there is an annex as large or larger than the main store. A person could walk into the Coop and buy everything from lingerie and clothing to school supplies, fabric and notions to books and records, footwear to jewelry. I've been known to spend half a day wandering from department to department.

An hour later, I walked out of the store with two big bags under my arms full of books, compact discs, and a few new clothes. The sun had gone down, but the weather hadn't turned any colder.

Shifting my new belongings in my arms, I walked to the T and rode home.

I dropped the roll of film off at a nearby drugstore and trudged back to my apartment. After I fixed myself some supper, I went back over the case and what I had learned. I came to the conclusion that I hadn't learned enough to determine who killed Tom Grady and why. The phone rang and I picked it up.

"Hello?"

"Angela? This is Sheilah. Sheilah Grady."

"Yeah, hi, Sheilah," I replied. "What's up? I bet you're calling to see what I have to report." *And to let me know that someone broke into your father's house,* I thought. But I decided to let her tell me that without prompting. It wouldn't be wise to tip my hand.

"I apologize for calling you at home, but yes, I'd like to know what you've found out so far." She didn't sound sorry to me. I let it pass.

"Well, I spent all day yesterday, and some of the evening, talking to possible witnesses to the murder," I said. I went on to tell Sheilah about my interviews at the Wild

Irish Rose Pub and the Goode Times Club. Then I told her about the witness.

"She saw your dad leaving the pub at the time everyone else claimed to see him leave," I explained, "but she also was able to remember a man walking after him."

"But wouldn't there be plenty of people out on the street at that hour?" Sheilah asked. I could almost hear the frown in her voice.

"Not necessarily," I replied. "It was about one, the witching hour in the Zone, the hour before the clubs closed down on a weekend night. Most people were staying with their choice of clubs. More drinking time if you're not out prowling the streets in search of a better time elsewhere."

"Mmm." She sounded less than enthusiastic.

Sensing that I might be turned loose before I had a chance to follow up my very slim leads, I quickly added, "I have a couple of pictures to show the witness in the Zone."

"What's the name of this witness?" she asked.

I thought it was curious that she'd want to know Eileen's identity—why should she care, as long as she gets results?

"I don't think it would be a good idea to tell you right now," I replied.

"Why not?" Sheilah asked, her voice strident. Didn't she believe me? Did she think I was making this up as I talked to her? She continued, "Are you sure you have a witness?" The suspicion in her voice was thick. I held my ground. I would not be bullied into giving out the name of a witness, even to my client, without permission. Besides, I had visions of Sheilah going down to the Combat Zone, confronting Eileen in the Exchange, and asking her a million questions. As amusing as the thought was, I didn't want to be responsible for my client's impulses.

"Yes, I'm sure I have a witness. I just can't tell you her name until I've spoken with her again. I'll have more information for you tomorrow."

But Sheilah Grady wouldn't let me off the phone. "Have you gone to my father's house yet? Have you found anything?" she asked eagerly.

I hesitated, waiting for her to tell me about the break-in. When she didn't say anything, I started to wonder if the Dorchester police had contacted her yet. I couldn't imagine that they hadn't.

"I was in Dorchester today," I admitted, "and only got to search the first floor."

"Only the first floor? You must have found something—"

"I heard someone at the back door," I interrupted. "Not someone with a key, if you know what I mean. I decided not to stick around to find out if they were friendly."

"Oh, my God," she said, "so it's true." For a moment I thought she was concerned for my safety, until she added, "So the house really was broken into. When the police called me, I thought it might have been you, so I wasn't alarmed."

"But you gave me a key," I pointed out. "Why would I want to break in through the back door when I could use the key to the front door?"

She sighed. "I thought maybe you'd misplaced the key, so you'd just smashed in a window. I've just been so mixed up since my father died. I'm sorry. Do you think they trashed the house?"

"I didn't stay to find out," I replied curtly. It was a small lie. I did have to walk down the stairs to leave by the front door, but I didn't linger at the scene. I added quickly, "I took a picture of you and Brian. For identification purposes." I knew it was the wrong thing to say the moment it left my mouth. I'm good at that.

"Identification? Of who, Brian? You can't be serious, Miss Matelli," she said. I noticed that we were back to formal names again. I made a mental note that it's never a good idea to get too chummy with the client. Sheilah's voice was chilly. "I can guarantee that my boyfriend is not the person who murdered my father."

"I know you think so, Miss Grady, but everyone is a suspect. I know you told me that you and Brian Scanlon watched movies the rest of that night, but—"

"He was with me all night long. We didn't go out at all."

"Yes, I guess I just wanted to check again." I decided to appease her. Arguing wouldn't do any good; it would only get me fired. "Look, I'll be going back to the house again in the next few days, but first I have a few other things to check on."

I spent a little more time soothing her ruffled feathers. Before hanging up the phone, I assured her that I had put everything aside to work exclusively on her case. Of course, I had no other cases at present, but I didn't mention that fact.

I stared into space for a few minutes after our conversation, trying to get it straight in my head what had to be done. Tomorrow was Friday. I would pick up the developed photos and work on putting names to the faces and feet of my burglars. That meant I would be spending some time at the offices of ILAP, maybe even talking to Seamus McRaney. It also meant I would have to think of a good cover story. I didn't think Mr. McRaney or his pals would be too happy to talk to a private detective. But maybe a journalist.

I picked up the phone and dialed Craig Cohen's home number. I wondered if I was interrupting a quiet evening at home with his family. I had no idea if he was married, single, living with someone, or what. A male voice answered. "Craig Cohen here."

"Craig? This is Angela Matelli."

"Hey, how you doing?" he said brightly. "Did you find any clues on the Grady case?"

"I think I've got a few leads and I need to follow them up. But I need a favor."

"Tell me," he said.

"I need to get into the ILAP offices. I don't want to use my real name or occupation, so I'll have to go as someone else. I thought a reporter would do nicely. I could use the name Janet Roberts," I said, biting my lip. "Can you back me up?"

There was just a slight hesitation. Then he replied, "Okay. But you have to do something for me."

"Anything within reason."

"See if you can get an interview with Seamus McRaney. Tape it for me."

I raised my eyebrows in surprise. "Sure, I'll try to get one. But why can't you call him up and make arrangements yourself?"

"He's very difficult to pin down. He has a public relations director do most of the interviews. My theory is that he tries to stay out of the limelight so questions about his background won't be asked."

"Because of his father."

"That's right," Craig replied. "McRaney doesn't need to be connected to the IRA, even indirectly."

"It must be hard having to pretend that your father doesn't exist," I said.

"Don't feel too sorry for Seamus McRaney, Angela," Craig said, his voice hard. "There's no solid proof, but from all the circumstantial evidence, he's his father's son."

# ♣ Chapter 15

When I hung up from talking to Craig, who assured me that he'd support my story, I realized how weary I was from two days of constant running around. I had opened my agency only last week and already needed a vacation.

I fell into bed after watching the late evening news on television. It seemed like I only closed my eyes for a minute when I was awakened by the shrill ringing of the phone. My hand clumsily felt around for the phone until I found the receiver.

"Hello?" I muttered. My eyes were so bleary that I couldn't focus on the alarm clock next to my bed.

"Back off," growled a sinister voice.

I was suddenly wide awake, sitting bolt upright in bed.

"Who is this?" I asked. Glancing at my clock, I did a double-take. It was three-thirty. Still slightly confused from waking up so abruptly, I looked at the light coming from the window, or the lack of light. I had been asleep for only a few hours and now I was being threatened over the phone. My hand started shaking.

"I said, back off the Grady case," the muffled voice demanded, "or someone could get hurt."

"What are you talking about?" I said. "Who could get hurt?" There was a click, then a buzz. *There's my answer,* I thought. *I'll be the one who gets hurt. Terrific.*

A trickle of cold sweat crept down my back. I stared into the receiver like it was going to tell me who had just scared the living daylights out of me. Just great. My first phone threat. I replayed the voice in my head, trying to latch on to an accent or something familiar, but I soon realized that it was useless. Whoever had called me had made sure that identification would be impossible.

I got up and padded over to the closet where I kept my baseball bat. My gun was still at the office. I brought it to bed with me. It was the most exciting thing I'd slept with in months.

Despite having my weapon of choice nestled in my arms, I didn't sleep much the rest of the night. Around six in the morning, an hour I had happily forgotten about since leaving the military, I got up and made myself a nice big breakfast. My trusty bat was propped up next to the stove.

I thought about that phone call all through breakfast. And I thought about the case while I showered and dressed. The more I thought about the phone call, the angrier I got. I hate being pushed around and I hate being threatened even more. By the time I was dressed, I was determined to find the son of a bitch who'd interrupted my sleep so I could pound his head in with my Louisville slugger.

By the time I was out the door and headed for Maverick Station at eight-thirty in the morning, I was envisioning the phone caller's trial and consequent prison sentence. I calmed down enough to remember the film at the drugstore just before I reached the turnstile. I trudged up the T station stairs again, went to the drugstore, picked up the film, paid for it, and stuffed the package in my purse.

By the time I got to the office, it was almost nine-thirty. There was another message from Ma, threatening me with bodily harm if I missed Sunday dinner this weekend. Great, I needed another ultimatum this morning.

I opened the envelope of photos and riffled through them. I hadn't done too badly. The focus was sharp and I'd gotten foot shots, head shots, and full body shots in a couple of the pictures. It was enough to recognize the burglars. I would have to go find Eileen sometime this weekend and show her the photos. It was ludicrous to think that she could make an identification, but my job was to run up every lead, including if they appeared absurd.

The phone rang and I picked it up, remembering to sound like a receptionist. "Angela Matelli Investigations. May I help you?"

It was Raina. She chided me for not calling earlier. "So, is the only time I ever see you going to be when you need a favor, Miss Big Shot?" she said in an airy tone.

"Sorry about that," I replied sheepishly. "Believe me, I haven't exactly been out living it up every night. What about you?"

She sighed. "Nightlife is a thing of the past. I've given up on meeting men in bars."

"I wish my sister would," I replied wistfully.

"Yeah, how is Sophia?"

"Evicted," I said shortly.

"Evicted?"

I told Raina the story, ending with, "So now she's moving in my building because the rent is the right price—cheap. I just hope she finds another place soon. I'd like to rent out that ground-floor apartment to someone nice." A light bulb went on over my head. Figuratively, of course. "Say, you wouldn't be interested . . ."

Raina laughed. "Not at the moment. I'm happy where I'm living."

Raina lived in a big house in Waltham, inherited from her parents. Her father had taken early retirement and Raina's parents were now living in Florida. Why would she want to give up all that luxury for a ground-floor one-bedroom in East Boston?

"Are you free for dinner tonight?" she asked.

I nodded enthusiastically into the receiver. "Yeah. Sounds great. Should we go out or what?"

We finally agreed that I'd cook my famous carbonara, she'd bring the wine, and we'd watch old movies for the rest of the night. Not exactly a hot date, but I didn't think I'd be up for the meat market scene.

I realized, after hanging up, that it was Friday and the weekend was almost upon me. Sunday at Ma's hung over me like a dark cloud. At the same time that I dreaded the prospect of spending time with Ma, I looked forward to a home-cooked meal. Ma could have been a master chef if she'd wanted to. But even a delicious meal sometimes didn't seem worth the scrutiny I had to endure.

I sighed and roused myself from the office chair. It was ten o'clock and Craig Cohen had by now called ILAP and paved the way for me by telling them that he was sending down a reporter. I had dressed specifically for the occasion, choosing dark gray, itchy wool slacks and a muted print blouse with a light gray blazer. I'd even found a couple of dark-colored barrettes from the back of my vanity drawer and used them to pull back my hair on either side.

When I'd finished dressing this morning at my apartment, I had studied myself in the full-length mirror. I had to admit that I looked pretty good, despite the fading bruises. I actually looked like a professional, a career journalist—maybe even like a Harvard graduate. I added my camera, a minicassette recorder, and a steno pad and pen.

I took the T to Harvard Square again and got there a little before eleven. When I walked in the door of the ILAP office, my first impression was that chaos really reigned. People were yelling across the room to each other, answering two or three lines at a time, the clack of typewriters a constant staccato in the background. I wondered why they hadn't computerized, then I noticed that several desks were equipped with computers, but I gathered that most of the correspondence was done by secretaries with typewriters.

I must have looked bewildered, because a short, pert, blond woman bounced up to me.

"Can I help you?" she asked in a perky voice.

I smiled and said, "I'm Janet Roberts with the *Globe*. My boss, Mr. Cohen, was supposed to call you this morning to let you know that I'd be coming in to do a story."

Her face brightened, if that was possible, and she replied, "Oh, yes. Tanya took the call. You'll be given a tour of the office by me and I'll answer all your questions. My name is Elizabeth Bright, but everyone calls me Bit. Excuse me a moment, there seems to be a problem with the computer over there." And she was off and running. I got the impression that she served as the public relations coordinator because of her bubbly personality.

I was wondering how I would endure the info-tour with this refugee from a light bulb factory when Seamus McRaney walked through the door. He was dressed better than when I'd first seen him at the Shandy. His dark blue suit, striped shirt, and red power tie hid a slender, lanky build and emphasized the shoulders and his handsome face. If I hadn't already known who he was, I might have mistaken him for a stockbroker. He was walking fast, his head down, so I maneuvered myself into his path and we collided.

"Eh? Oh, excuse me, miss," he started to apologize; then looked up at me for the first time. I could see the little wheels turning in his head as he realized that I was not part of the great ILAP machine. "Miss—?"

This was my cue and I grabbed it. "Roberts. Janet Roberts." I stayed close to him. In fact, I found myself magnetically drawn to his blue eyes. I had enough sense to stick out my hand.

He shook hands. "Eh, Seamus McRaney here."

I feigned surprise and awe. "Not *the* Seamus McRaney. The one who founded the International League for the Advancement of Peace?"

"Aye. The very one. Can I help you with something? I know you're not part of the staff." He grinned impishly for emphasis and added, "Not yet, anyway."

I looked around, sweeping my free hand in a wide gesture to take everything in, and lightly asked, "How can you tell? There are so many people here."

"I know all my people. I have met every single one of them." He cocked his head to the side and said, "But tell me, Miss Roberts, what brings you here? Are you perhaps looking for something worthy to invest your time in?"

I laughed, charmed by his accent and his smile. "No, I'm a reporter for the *Globe*. I'm here to do a story on ILAP."

A small hand grabbed my shoulder. "There you are!" said Bit, shooting an accusing look at me. "I'm terribly sorry, Seamus, but I had a crisis to deal with. I didn't know she would accost you—"

He smiled and patted her shoulder in a fatherly gesture. "That's all right, Bit." He turned to me and said,

"I've enjoyed our talk, Miss Roberts. Perhaps you'll allow me to buy you lunch after your tour. I could answer a few more of your questions."

I tried not to beam with pleasure because Seamus McRaney was taking me to lunch, but I could tell from some of the reactions of some of the office workers within hearing distance that this was something special. I nodded and replied, "I'd be delighted. It would give my article a personal touch, being able to add a few words from the founder of ILAP."

"Then it's a date," he replied, his eyes sparkling as he walked off.

Bit apologized for having been so sharp a moment earlier. "We're in the middle of getting ready for the St. Patrick's Day Rally on Sunday," she said in a confidential tone.

I tried to look understanding. "Good heavens!" I replied. "Is it the middle of March already? Where is this parade going to take place?"

"Briggs Field at MIT," Bit replied enthusiastically. "Seamus is going to make a speech at the rally."

She led me on the tour, hurrying through a lecture that was so mechanical and dull that I would have preferred to read a copy of the prepared speech. I learned about the cold-calling department, a group of volunteers who made phone calls to companies and individuals who had contributed previously to other worthy causes. And then there was the envelope stuffer department, more volunteers who ran off hundreds of fliers pleading for money. I was also whisked through the area where people were preparing for Sunday's St. Patrick's Day activities, making green tissue carnations with a tag that read, "Faith and Begorrah! Thank you for your donation."

Bit and I were old pals by then. She bounced around the office, giving me perky speeches about the good work that was being done to help political prisoners in Northern Ireland and how many Irish-Americans were already contributing to the cause.

We passed a closed door. Curious, I pointed to it and asked, "What's in there?"

She hesitated, her face closing up as tight as the door, and said, "Oh, that's just storage space for office supplies." Bit hustled me along.

I looked back at the door. We had passed an office supply closet earlier. It was hard for me to believe that there were two closets where they kept extra paper, pens, envelopes, and printer ribbons. But I didn't argue.

We finally arrived at Seamus McRaney's office. It was much more grandiose than the rest of the place. A glass wall had been installed when the office had been built. Seamus could look out at his busy little volunteers whenever he wanted to. At the moment, full drapes had been drawn to close it off and give him some privacy.

Bit turned to me confidentially and said in a hushed, awe-filled voice, "This is where Seamus does his work. You're very lucky to get a personal interview. He usually doesn't give them."

"Who usually does?" I asked.

"Tanya. She's our public relations director. Seamus saves himself for all the big speeches, like the one he's going to give at the rally on Sunday."

*Great,* I thought, *I didn't even rate Tanya when Craig called to set up this phony interview.*

"Why doesn't Mr. McRaney give interviews? He seems personable enough and very charming."

Bit screwed up her face like she was six years old and started biting her fingernails. I found her habits to be uncomfortably childlike. She replied, "He likes his privacy. If someone else can handle the media for him, he's all for it."

Bit instructed me to wait by her desk while she went into the office to let Seamus know I was done with my tour. I looked around and caught sight of the two men whose pictures I'd taken the day before. Bit was still in the office, so I grabbed a passing volunteer wearing a Harvard sweatshirt.

"Say, you wouldn't be able to tell me who that guy with the red beard is, could you?" I pointed to the man with the blue and white running shoes.

The girl adjusted her glasses, squinted in the direction of my finger, then bobbed her head. "Oh, yeah. That's Liam O'Kelly. He's the associate director of ILAP."

"And what about the fellow standing next to him, the tall good-looking one?" I pointed out the guy wearing black motorcycle boots. Seeing him up close, I noticed that he was a big, ruggedly handsome guy.

I turned back to the girl. She eyed the tall, handsome Irishman longingly and sighed. "Isn't he gorgeous? His name's Eammon O'Driscoll."

I asked, "What does he do around here?"

My question got her attention. "I'm not sure what he does," she said, "but he's from Belfast and hangs around Seamus and Liam."

I thanked her. Bit came out of the office. "Seamus will be out shortly," she said. Then she dashed by me, throwing a quick wave over her shoulder.

A minute passed and McRaney still hadn't come out of his office. I started wandering around, working toward the closed door I'd asked about earlier. I tried the handle.

"You won't get far," a voice said, startling me.

I turned around. Seamus McRaney stood just a foot away. My heart jumped into my throat, but I managed a small smile.

"What do you mean?" I asked.

"Why, it's locked," he replied, grinning. He held up a

key, brushed past me, unlocked it, and flung the door open. It was full of office supplies—computer monitors, printers, typewriters, and so on. Not for the first time, I felt stupid for my suspicions. What did I think I would find there, a gun cache, or perhaps a secret meeting room for the IRA? I hoped I wasn't blushing.

"As you can see," Seamus was saying, "we've been blessed with many contributions. So many, in fact, that we had to store some of them. We lock them up so no one will be tempted to steal them."

"Why do you still use typewriters? It looks like you could put together at least three more computers, from what I see in here."

Seamus shrugged. "We try to use everyone's contribution. Some of our older volunteers are more comfortable with typewriters, which we use for personal correspondence. I guess I'm just kind of old-fashioned."

"Which do you use," I asked, "typewriter or computer?"

He grinned. "Now, there you've got me. I've got both a typewriter and a computer in my office. A little of the old, a little of the new." He locked the closet again and we started to walk out. "Where would you like to have lunch?"

I gave him my best smile and said, "Surprise me."

We went around the corner to a German restaurant and were seated immediately. Seamus ordered a dark German beer and bratwurst; I ordered sauerbraten and a dark brew as well.

"I thought Irishmen only drank Guinness," I said.

"Ah, you don't know us well, then." He grinned. "You know, stout isn't the only drink in Ireland."

"Oh?" My beer was placed in front of me and I took a sip.

"There's lager and lime, and then there's the shandy."

I managed not to choke on my ale. "The shandy?" I feigned innocence and asked, "Isn't that a pub in Cambridge?"

Raising his eyebrows, he nodded. "I'll have to take you there sometime."

"So it was named after a drink," I mused. "Tell me what a shandy is."

Seamus leaned forward. I had to admit that he was very charismatic. I had to keep reminding myself that I was here trying to learn something for my investigation. It was hard to imagine that this man could be a terrorist.

"A shandy is a mixture of a light ale and a sparkling lemonade drink," he explained, "similar to your Seven-up or Sprite."

I made a face.

Seamus laughed and said, "No, really. It's a thirst-quencher, especially on a hot summer day. I've learned to enjoy it with ice here in your country."

I grimaced and said, "I think I'll stick to beer." I hoisted my glass and sipped it. Seamus looked on with amusement.

Our meal arrived and we talked over lunch. When we were almost done, I turned to him and said, "You know, this was supposed to be an interview."

Seamus shrugged, a sheepish expression on his face as he explained, "For me, it was a way of getting a pretty girl to share lunch with me. But I'll be happy to answer a few of your questions, if you like."

I turned on my recorder, took out my notepad and pencil, and said, "There's been a lot of controversy over the goals of ILAP. Some people say we should stay out of other countries' business when it comes to political prisoners."

Seamus passed a hand over his chin, which was covered with dark stubble. "Well, I guess if we all stayed out of each other's business, Nelson Mandela would still be in prison and maybe even Lech Walesa. Governments would stagnate. People would continue to live under the domination of such monsters as Ceausescu."

I began to write, scribbling my own brand of short-hand. I was actually taking notes, but mostly on his appearance and his manner. "How can you equate a great black leader like Mandela with men who are considered, by many people the world over, to be Irish Republican Army terrorists in Belfast?" I asked.

He didn't even hesitate to think that one out. He must have been asked that same question many times over. "How do you know those prisoners are terrorists?" he shot back.

"Well, I've read it in—"

"The papers," he finished. "You're a journalist. You should know that not everything you read is the absolute truth. What has been written about the IRA may be partially true, but you never know the whole story until you've heard both sides, right?"

"In other words," I said, "to get the full picture, I have to listen with an unbiased ear."

He leaned back in his seat and said, "Exactly."

"Then are you telling me that you're in league with the IRA?" I knew that question was going to get me in trouble.

Seamus McRaney fixed his blue eyes on me. I felt my knees go weak. It took all my effort to focus on breathing normally. "I'm on everyone's side," he answered evenly. "I believe in freedom of speech and freedom of politics. I also believe all of Ireland will one day be free from the rule of our oppressor, Great Britain."

"Do you believe in the freedom to kill innocent by-standers?" I asked, then went on to explain, "I read about the twelve who were killed in Dublin the other day.

The IRA claimed responsibility for the deed. Is this the action of sane people?"

Seamus frowned. "I seem to recall reading about that incident. Of course I don't believe in killing innocent people. No sane person would." He touched my hand. "Please don't equate my organization with that radical group. It's not good for our image."

"Then what was the purpose of the bomb?" I persisted.

He shook his head. "You're asking me to think like a terrorist. But I might be able to answer it in part. I think some people become so frustrated with the politics of their country that they begin thinking in convoluted terms such as: If we plant bombs in the center of Dublin and they go off at five o'clock when people are getting out of work, maybe the random violence will wake people up to the violence in Belfast."

I raised my eyebrows. "That may make sense to a few people, but I still don't understand it."

"And you will continue to not understand until it's your friend who is killed or until you yourself are in jeopardy."

I noticed that he'd kept his hand near mine, which I found distracting. He was attractive and I was starting to fervently wish that he wasn't even remotely involved with my case.

I changed the subject slightly. "I know a little about random violence. About a week ago, a friend of mine was killed in the Combat Zone. He had gone to a pub for a few drinks. When he left, he was assaulted and stabbed. The police think it was a random killing, but there are those who think it was premeditated."

I was looking for a reaction, some sign of guilt, but if Seamus McRaney was party to Tom Grady's death, he was very good at hiding it. He didn't even blink.

Instead, he nodded, looking very serious, and asked, "Why do you believe that?"

"Well, there were some extenuating circumstances regarding his death, things only a few people know." I was being deliberately vague. I didn't want to accuse him of being connected to Grady's death when I had no proof. If Seamus McRaney was tied up in the murder, it was dangerous enough for me to bring it up.

I changed the subject. "Has the fact that your father was a member of the IRA affected your work with ILAP?"

I had expected a big reaction, but instead, Seamus looked down for a moment, then met my eyes and said, "My father's death will always affect me personally. There isn't a day that goes by that I don't think about him. As for ILAP, well, it's brought up sometimes, and of course there is speculation—like father, like son. But his death made me realize that we have to work together to free people through peaceful means. All of us. Violence doesn't solve anything."

It was a touching speech, but extremely canned. Even I didn't fall for it.

"But a moment ago," I pointed out, "you were just telling me about the IRA, almost to the point of defending its methods."

Seamus stood up and collected the check. "My beliefs are separate from my father's beliefs. But I grew up with him and I understand his way of thinking and, consequently, how IRA members think. That doesn't mean I agree with those ideals."

"Tell me about the men who work with you. What does Liam O'Kelly do? And Eammon O'Driscoll, what is his title?"

These were questions that caught him off guard. Seamus blinked, then collected himself and smiled at me.

"My, you do your homework, don't you?"

I returned his smile, trying to look as cool and collected as possible.

"Liam is my assistant director," he said. "He oversees the operation of the temporary workers and liaisons with city officials to make sure any rally we have is fully approved and licensed. And he finds people within the city who are willing to work on a temporary basis to connect with the media for us."

"That's an awful lot to do. And what is Eammon O'Driscoll's job?"

He hesitated for a moment, then replied, "He's my speechwriter."

I looked skeptical. He explained, "Both Liam and Eammon are childhood friends. We grew up in the violence of Belfast. We work together to try and help the unfortunates of our city."

"Does that include those who have British blood? Those who are Protestant? Those who might not believe in freedom for Northern Ireland?"

Seamus kept his eyes fixed on my face. I thought I detected anger in those cool blue eyes, but he kept his features carefully controlled. "We help anyone who comes to us for aid. We distribute the funds equitably."

*Oh, he's good,* I thought. "I understand that you have a few Irish-Americans who contribute to your cause," I said. "Is it difficult to get them to send you money?"

"Not at all," he replied, visibly relaxing at the change in subject. "Many of them love the old country and are happy to help the cause." Seamus McRaney wielded the words "old country" like a club. Those were probably the operative words when dealing with Irish-Americans who wanted to help their distant Irish relations.

"My uncle was a cop who worked with quite a few Irishmen. Do many Irish-American law enforcement officers contribute, or are they naturally more suspicious of your motives than the average Irish-American?"

"Policemen tend to be more careful about what causes they donate to, of course," Seamus said. "Most of them will investigate a cause before sending in their contributions, but we do get a few contributions from that sector of society."

I pressed on. "The man who died recently was one of my uncle's very good friends, Tom Grady. He was thinking of contributing," I lied, "but he died before he could do so."

Seamus frowned. "I'm sorry to hear that. We have a member of our organization named Sheilah Grady whose father died recently. Was that her father?"

"Yes. His funeral was last Tuesday," I said, then added, "I thought I saw you there."

He raised his eyebrows and shook his head. "You must be mistaken, Miss Roberts," he said in a frosty voice. "I was at a meeting. I didn't know the man personally."

I was surprised that he had such a distinct reaction to my comment. I was certain I'd seen him there. Why would he lie about something like that?

I turned the recorder off and put my notebook and pencil away in my purse. Seamus McRaney certainly was a convincing speaker, very persuasive, very smooth. I wanted to believe that he had no ties to the IRA beyond his father's connection. I wanted to believe that he had nothing but the best of intentions. But I also knew that when someone appeared to be too good to be true, he probably was.

We strolled back to the office and lingered by the door. Suddenly I heard, "Angela! What are you doing here?"

I looked around and came face-to-face with Brian Scanlon. His face was like a thundercloud. He turned to

Seamus and calmly asked, "What have you been telling her?"

Seamus McRaney didn't ruffle easily. Instead, he eyed me with curiosity and said, "Angela, eh? I thought your name was Janet." He said to Brian, "I've been telling her about the goals of our organization, of course. Is she some sort of spy? Why would she want to do that?"

I was tempted to start slinking away or to sink into the earth, but I stood my ground and stayed sullenly silent.

"What did she tell you?" Brian demanded of McRaney, ignoring his questions. I felt like a piece of furniture.

"That she was a journalist for the *Globe*. She told me her name was Janet Roberts."

Brian snorted. "Her name is Angela Matelli. She's a private detective, working for my girlfriend."

Seamus lifted a finger, shook it, and said, "Don't tell me. Sheilah, right? And her father was Tom Grady." He looked at me for confirmation.

I nodded.

Seamus looked at me with renewed interest. "Private detective, eh? You're too pretty to be doing such dirty work."

I gritted my teeth. Any interest I'd had in Seamus McRaney had disappeared with that last comment. I was sorely tempted to hit him, but being a lady, I refrained. Instead, I replied, "Somebody's gotta do it."

There was an amused twinkle in his eye. He remained civilized, shaking my hand and saying, "Well, it certainly was a pleasure meeting you, Miss . . . Matelli, is it? I hope you got some helpful information, although I haven't the foggiest notion what this was all about."

If Brian's eyes had been lasers, they could have burned holes through my clothes. In a low, even voice, he said, "I think you're finished here. I'll be talking to you later."

The only response I could come up with was a smirk. Then I spun on my heel and walked away.

# ♣ Chapter 16

*I'm an idiot, I'm an idiot, I'm an idiot* was my mantra all the way home. I didn't bother to stop at my office. I was tempted to go ahead and finish the job all in one night. The only leads I had to follow up were continuing the search of Grady's house and heading back to the Combat Zone to show Eileen the photos I'd taken.

If I hadn't received a threatening call and my office hadn't been tossed, I might think Tom Grady's murder *had* been just a mugging. Some memory in the back of my mind nagged at me, something that related to Tom Grady's death, and possibly to my mugging. But I just couldn't get hold of it. *Maybe if I relaxed,* I thought, *I'd recall it.*

Then I remembered that I had a dinner to fix tonight for Raina. By the time I transferred at Park Street, I was in such a foul mood, I considered calling her up for a rain check. But I needed some R and R. I'd been on this case since Wednesday morning and I hadn't stopped long enough to do more than get home late, fix a quick dinner, then get some sleep. But tonight I'd enjoy myself, even if it was only a quiet dinner and rented movies with my childhood friend.

When I got to Maverick Square, I picked up the items I needed for a good carbonara, plus lettuce and a loaf of Italian bread. I got home a little before five. After putting my purchases in the kitchen, I dialed Craig Cohen's work number. I caught him as he was getting ready to leave.

"How did it go?" he asked.

"I got your interview," I replied, "but you'll have to judge how good it is for yourself." I took a deep breath and said, "And I have a couple more names for you. Can you run them down and let me know what you come up with?"

"Sure," he said. "Let me call up the file." There were a few moments of quiet, with only the sound of a keyboard clicking in the background. "Shoot," he said.

I gave him Liam and Eammon's names, then waited a few more minutes while his computer beeped and blipped. Finally he replied, "I'm getting some information on O'Driscoll, but nothing on O'Kelly. Maybe that's not his real name. I'll keep working on it."

"What about O'Driscoll?" I asked. My free hand, I noticed, had become a tense fist.

"His profile is sketchy, but Eammon O'Driscoll is an alias. His real name is Eaonn Daley. Maybe the police have more on file, but the one thing I can tell you is that O'Driscoll's wanted for questioning in Northern Ireland regarding a bombing about a year ago. He's managed to evade British and Irish authorities and Interpol. You say he's here in Boston?"

"He's posing as Seamus McRaney's speechwriter," I replied dryly.

"You should contact the police or the FBI," Craig warned me. "Don't approach this guy yourself."

I sighed and asked, "And there's nothing on a Liam O'Kelly?"

"Not in my files," he said. "Maybe you should get in

touch with someone who has some experience with terrorists, especially IRA terrorists. My contact is out of town on vacation, but I could—"

I cut him off. "Thanks, Craig. I appreciate your help. I think I've got enough information for right now. I'll call you after the weekend and get that taped interview to you. Then we can talk."

"I can be reached anytime this weekend," he replied, "if you need to talk to me. And Angie," Craig added, his tone getting serious, "I'm serious about contacting the authorities. O'Driscoll, and probably O'Kelly, are dangerous. You don't want to approach them without backup."

"Don't worry about me," I replied lightly. "I have no intention of doing so. And when the time is right, I'll let the police know."

I thanked him again for his help. Then we hung up.

I opened one of my latest purchases, a new John Hiatt CD, popped it into the CD player, and turned the volume up. Then I went into the kitchen to prepare dinner. Raina showed up a little after six. I was working on the third time through the Hiatt CD.

"Sounds good," she said, stepping into my kitchen. She drew a bottle of white wine out of a paper sack, followed by a carton of coffee fudge ice cream. I gave her a look that could kill. She raised her arms in mock protection and took a step back. "I couldn't help it," she replied in defense. "It was calling to me." I opened a cupboard door to reveal one of my vices, white cheddar cheese popcorn. We grinned at each other like two maniacs.

The carbonara turned out terrific, and Raina's choice of movies, *The Tall Guy* and *Hairspray*, were entertaining. Both of us liked to rent the smaller releases because it was less likely that we'd gone to see them in the theaters.

Raina told me how work was going, and I told her as

much about the Grady case as I could get away with, including my threatening phone call and the humiliating experience of being "made" this afternoon.

"Ouch," Raina said with a wince. "So what about this phone call? Doesn't it worry you?" she asked, reaching for the bowl of popcorn. I was still stuffed from dinner. I didn't understand how my skinny friend could pack away as much as she did.

I wrinkled my nose and said, "Well, yeah. It does. The guy didn't call me at my office, he called me at home. That means he knows where I live. I'll have to be careful for the next few days."

"So what do you think is going to happen?" she asked, grabbing a handful of kernels.

I shrugged and sighed. "Considering what happened this afternoon, I'll probably get fired. But as far as I'm concerned, I'm still on the case until further notice."

As if on cue, the phone rang. I looked at Raina. Her eyes widened. I got up and answered, "Hello."

"Brian Scanlon here." His voice was cold and flat. I tried to place it as the threatening voice that woke me this morning at three-thirty, but I'd been so groggy, I didn't think I could positively identify it.

"Hello, Mr. Scanlon," I said, attempting to sound as if nothing had happened this afternoon. "What can I do for you?"

"You stay away from Sheilah from now on. And ILAP."

"Is that a threat?" I asked sweetly, adding, "Like the call I got this morning?"

"What are you talking about?" he asked gruffly. "I've never called you before in my life."

"I don't understand why you're so upset," I said.

Scanlon replied, "You come into ILAP, asking questions about me—"

"I never asked questions about you. I already know enough—"

He interrupted my interruption. "Okay, you didn't ask any questions about me, but you're jeopardizing my relationship with Sheilah and my friendship with Seamus McRaney."

"I'm not interested in Seamus McRaney. I'm interested in Liam and Eammon and where they were on Thursday morning—"

"You're off this case, so just drop it, okay?" he said shortly. "I talked to Sheilah and she agrees that it would be best to drop the whole thing. She's beginning to think it was just an unfortunate accident that her father was mugged and killed."

"Anything you say," I said blithely. "But would it be all right if I talked to Sheilah—"

He cut me off. "No. She doesn't want to talk to you. You'll be getting your termination notice by mail. Sheilah will see to it tomorrow morning." He hung up before I had a chance to say anything else. Of course, any explanation of my actions would just have been a desperate attempt to convince him that I had a hot lead, which would have been a lie.

I went back into the living room. Raina had eaten half the bowl of popcorn already. I plopped down on the couch next to her, let out a big sigh, then said, "You heard?"

"From listening to your part of the conversation, it didn't sound like you were winning any popularity contest with the boyfriend."

With my finger, I lazily traced invisible patterns on the leg of my jeans. "Well, I guess I wasn't cut out to be a civilian investigator. Maybe I should join up for a few more years."

Raina laughed loudly. "I remember the letters I used

to get from you complaining about the regulations and strict codes you had to go by. Especially the hours. You hate to wake up that early in the morning! I don't think so." She sat up and leaned over to give my hand a squeeze. "This is only your first case. And it was a tough one. From what you've told me, and what I've read in the files at the station, there's no proof that Grady was more than the victim of a random mugging."

I sat up and said, "But I was mugged that night, too. It's possible that someone knew that I was peripherally involved in this case, someone who knows Sheilah and Brian and Seamus and the International League for the Advancement of Peace."

"Someone like those two burglars you almost met in Tom Grady's house?"

I nodded vigorously. Then my shoulders slumped. "And there's something that keeps slipping away from me, some piece of information that may have something to do with my mugging and Grady's death. But I can't seem to grasp it. And now I'm off the case."

Raina was silent for a minute. She finally said, "Who hired you?"

I looked up. "Sheilah Grady."

She looked at me steadily. "And who fired you?"

"Sheilah."

"But did she actually come on the phone and tell you she didn't want you on the case anymore?"

"No, it was Scanlon," I said. Raina's point hit home. I sat up and, almost talking to myself, added, "And she won't be sending out that termination notice until tomorrow, Saturday, which means I probably won't get it until Monday, maybe Tuesday, if I don't go into the office and open my mail." A grin spread across my face. "So I have two, maybe three days more to investigate. And she certainly paid me enough of a retainer to cover that much time." I grabbed the popcorn bowl away from her and began munching, saying through a mouthful, "Raina, you're a genius."

Raina smiled modestly.

She left around midnight. I had an early day tomorrow. Before I got ready for bed, I wanted to make sure I still knew where the key to Grady's house was. I pulled my purse onto my lap and began searching. I took out the photo of Brian and Sheilah. It could still come in handy when I found Eileen at the Exchange. I looked inside my purse and spotted the ILAP brochure, the one I'd taken from Grady's desk.

*Why ever did I take it?* I thought. I took it out and began thumbing through it. Just about all the information I'd gotten from Bit during the tour was contained in here. I stared at it, willing it to reveal the secret.

The phone rang, and I jumped off of the couch. I picked it up on the second ring, wondering who would be calling me at this time of night.

"Hello."

"Angie? Sophia."

*Of course,* I thought. "How thoughtful of you to call me after midnight," I said dryly.

"Everyone stays up late on a Friday night," she replied. "Besides, this was the only time my boss would let me use the phone."

"What do you want?" It was a rude question, but Sophia never brought out the best in me anyway. But she was hard to offend.

"I got the key from Rosa," she said, "and I'll be moving in over the weekend, both Saturday and Sunday."

"Fine." I dreaded what was coming next. Maybe I'm psychic, but my prediction was probably due to the fact that I'd lived with Sophia for over fifteen years and had known her a total of twenty-nine years.

"Say, are you free on Sunday?" she asked brightly. "I'll be moving in a few basic things tomorrow, but I'll need some help on Sunday."

"I don't know," I hedged. I knew it, she wanted me to help her move.

"Well, if you find the time, I could use the help."

"I thought you'd be rounding up a couple of the guys from the bar where you work. Don't you have any biker boyfriends at the moment?" I asked, but my sarcasm sailed right past Sophia.

"Not at the moment," she replied. "But I found a few friends who'll help me. If you have the time, we won't turn you away. If not, I think I've got enough people who have promised to help."

"Sounds good," I replied. "I may or may not be there. I have a case to work on this weekend."

"This weekend? Oh, come on, Angie. No one, except barmaids like me, works on the weekends. Admit it, you just don't want to help your big sister," she said, laughing.

"Well, not this private eye," I replied grimly. "We don't know the meaning of weekends. And I honestly would like to help if I have the time tomorrow or Sunday."

"Well, don't forget Ma on Sunday."

I groaned. "I don't know if I'll be able to make it again."

"She won't like that," Sophia said ominously.

"Thanks for your support, sis," I replied.

After we hung up, I climbed into bed, still thinking about the ILAP pamphlet I'd found in Tom Grady's house and what it could mean. At least it gave me more of a reason to go back to Dorchester. There might be another clue hidden somewhere.

That night, I had a nightmare. I was stuck under a bed,

while dozens of blue and white running shoes and black motorcycle boots passed by. I didn't know why I was hiding, but I just knew it was a good idea. Just as they were about to discover my hiding place, I woke up.

I sat up in bed, thirsty, sweat pouring out of every cell in my body. I went back over my dream, trying to untangle the meaning. Was there a meaning? I didn't know. But I did know that the last thing I saw in my dream before I was about to be discovered was Seamus McRaney's face. And I remembered the one word uttered just before I woke up. "Bomb!" The IRA—just the sort of folks I wanted to get involved with. I would probably be checking my car thoroughly every time I decided to drive it from now on. I shuddered at the ugly thoughts that were racing through my head.

The luminescent dial of my bedside clock showed the ungodly hour of four in the morning. I lay back on my pillow with my arms propped under my neck and tried to get back to sleep.

## ♣ *Chapter 17*

*I* was up at six-thirty again. I seemed to be back on an early morning schedule whether I liked it or not. I was starving; I guess nightmares can give a girl an appetite. After a hearty breakfast, I showered and dressed in jeans, sneakers, T-shirt, and pullover sweater.

When I stepped outside, I noticed that the weather was unusually warm. It had been raining, which was the first indication that spring was coming to New England. The first half of March had gone by, so the season was arriving just about on time.

I had decided to use the car again. But before I got in it, I checked under the hood and under the frame of the car. Then I inspected the taillights and headlights for any evidence of tampering. I wondered if I was just being cautious or if I was acting paranoid.

Seven-thirty is a nice, early hour on a Saturday morning and I figured that Route One would be free of traffic tangles and slowdowns. By arriving in Dorchester early, I was hoping to avoid Brian and Sheilah. I didn't know if they'd been to the house since my run-in with Liam and Eammon, and I didn't know if they were planning to spend Saturday sorting through her father's possessions, but I didn't want to take the chance of running into them. The longer I stayed out of contact with them, the better my chances were of discovering something concrete about Tom Grady's death.

On my way to Dorchester, it occurred to me that I hadn't been in touch with Detective Randolph lately. I felt guilty about not giving him what little information I had, but the clues I'd gathered so far were pretty weak. I resolved to call him when I had some solid evidence.

Dorchester was quiet. There were a few cars parked on Sullivan Drive, but no one was out on a day like this. This time, I parked my little green Datsun in front of Grady's house and went up the walkway as if I belonged there.

When I got inside and closed the door, I went straight to the back door to see what damage had been done. Someone had patched the broken pane in the door with a piece of cardboard and some tacks. *Well, that's going to discourage burglars from entering,* I thought. It was obvious from looking around that Sheilah hadn't visited the house yet.

I walked into the study. The thieves had left a bigger mess than when I had searched through it. At least I had taken the books off the shelves and stacked them neatly, intending to put them back when I was finished.

The books were now scattered over the brown carpet, many of them flung into far corners of the room. Papers from the desk drawers had been tossed carelessly everywhere. Pictures had been ripped from the walls and taken out of their frames. I found it odd that Sheilah hadn't been here yet to assess the damage, considering that she now knew that I hadn't been the burglar.

I'd been through the study before, but this time I was looking for Grady's address book. It crossed my mind that the burglars might have taken it, but I started the search anyway.

I was surprised to find the address book under a pile of typewritten sheets. I crouched to move the heap aside, then picked up the book and thumbed through it for a name I might recognize. Nothing. I looked through the rest of the book, but came up empty.

I rocked back on my heels. Maybe I was making it too difficult. It was very hot in Grady's house. The thermostat was probably still set for colder weather. I had a sudden, overwhelming need for a glass of water. I walked into the kitchen, got a glass, and opened the freezer. While pulling out an ice cube tray, it hit me like a ton of icicles—Grady had busted a dealer and found a stash in the freezer—in the ice cube trays.

The ice trays were the old-fashioned metal kind with the detached cube separators. I inspected them for evidence of something there, but a thick coating of frost on the cubes made it too difficult. I put the trays in the sink and ran hot water over them.

When the ice had melted, I found a small plastic bag in the bottom of one of the trays. When I held it up to the light, there was a slim three-by-five notebook inside. I opened the bag and slid it out. The pages were slightly damp, but I was able to flip through them quickly. The writing was still legible. A shiver of excitement ran up my spine.

Pocketing the notebook, I filled the trays with water and slid them back into the freezer section. Since I'd found what I was looking for, there was no need to search any further. I wanted to get out as quickly as possible. I locked up the house, got in my car, and drove back to East Boston.

Back in my apartment, seated on my sofa, I studied the notebook. The writing was cramped and hard to read, almost as if it were shorthand. Tom Grady had probably spent so many years quickly jotting down statements from witnesses in his notebook that his writing had degenerated. I would have to call in someone to decipher it. The only person I knew who had been on the force with Grady was "No-Legs" Charlie. I dialed his number.

"Yeah," the gruff voice on the other end of the line said.

"Hey, Uncle Charlie. It's me, Angie," I replied.

"Angela! Good to hear from you." His voice perked up. "So what've you been doing with yourself? You catch any crooks yet?"

I laughed. "No, but I'm working on it. Say, you heard about Tom Grady, right?"

"Terrible thing," he answered softly. "I'll miss him. Did he ever go to you about that job?"

"Yes—actually, I'm working for his daughter now. She wants me to find his killer."

My uncle grunted. "I hope you're not going to spend too much time on that one. It sounds like a wild goose chase to me."

I explained, in detail, some of the things that had happened over the last week, including my mugging, Sheilah's boyfriend, the ILAP, and the notebook I'd found that morning.

"So you want me to have a look at it?" he asked.

We agreed to meet at Santarpio's for lunch in an hour. I hung up, feeling like I was finally getting somewhere. After my uncle translated it, I would have to turn the notebook over to Detective Randolph, if there was anything in it worth turning over.

Santarpio's is an East Boston landmark. Located in between the Maverick Square Station and the Airport T Station on Chelsea Street, near an overpass, it was a family-owned bar and restaurant that had been around since

I was a child. Anticipating a Santarpio's pizza, I got there fifteen minutes early.

"No-Legs" Charlie was a regular there. He stopped in most days to visit with his other retired friends from the East Boston neighborhood. They usually had a few beers and played pinball in the back room.

I walked into the dark front room and let my eyes adjust. Everything in Santarpio's was old: the tables and chairs, the plates and flatware, the bar, and the bartender. The bar stood to the right of the entrance. I noticed several men from the neighborhood were perched on stools, a mug of beer or a glass of red wine in front of them. There were a few families seated at tables to the left, but the back room was deserted. The bartender, a guy named Joey, spotted me and called out, "Hey, Angie. You lookin' for your uncle? He's in the kitchen tellin' the chefs how to do their job."

I groaned. My uncle couldn't keep his opinions to himself. He had to tell everyone else how to run their business when he should have been minding his own. I gave Joey a friendly wave and went back to the kitchen.

It was a small white room with an enormous oven, a grill, and lots of table space in the center for chopping vegetables and meats, flipping dough, and assembling pizzas. There was more than pizzas on the menu, but when I ate there, I got their specialty. The dough was made with hard-milled flour so the crust baked up thin and crisp, the sauce was made from fresh tomatoes, and all their toppings came from local meat markets and greengrocers.

Two of the cooks were busy preparing meals for the customers. They nodded to me as I entered, but ignored the row going on in the center of the kitchen. Uncle Charlie sat in his wheelchair, pointing a butcher knife at the third cook, an older man named Artie, short for Arturio.

"Don't you come in here telling me how to cut my pizza toppings," Artie shouted, picking up a long sharp bread knife and shaking it. "I've been doing this longer than you were on the force. I didn't tell you how to be a policeman, did I?"

"All I want," Uncle Charlie shouted back, "is thicker slices of pepperoni. Just slice it thick again, the way you used to."

The cook brandished his knife. I winced a little, but I knew they wouldn't hurt each other. They'd been friends too long.

"I haven't changed the way I slice my pepperoni or any of my sausages," bellowed the cook. "That hasn't changed in thirty years!"

I decided this was a good time to step in. Uncle Charlie looked ridiculous wielding a knife. I deftly disarmed him. He looked up in astonishment, which turned into a smile.

"Angie. You're early. Artie and I have been discussing thick versus thin pepperoni slices. Which do you like better? Don't you think his pepperoni has been a little on the thin side lately?"

"Angie!" Artie appealed to me. "Get your uncle out of here before I slice him up." I thought I saw Artie wink slyly in my direction and I grinned.

Turning to my uncle, I tried my best to look disgusted, and said, "So this is how you waste your time, badgering Artie when he's got customers to feed. You need something to take your mind off food." I turned to Artie and said, "One large pizza with green peppers, mushrooms, onions, and hot peppers."

My uncle grabbed his stomach and groaned, saying, "Angie, you know hot peppers give me indigestion. And I'd rather have pepperoni on it."

I grinned and replied, "Make that with hot peppers on only half the pizza." I said to my uncle, "You know pepperoni isn't on your diet, thick or thin sliced."

"Ah, you're tryin' to kill me with this diet thing. Every once in a while—"

I threw "No-Legs" Charlie a stern look. "I'd be willing to bet that every once in a while is a lot more often. We're having a vegetarian pizza and that's the end of it. The cheese is enough fat for you."

He put his hands up in mock surrender. "Fine. Let's go grab a table."

Artie had put his knife down and was grabbing a handful of dough out of a large vat. "Which half do you want me to put the hot peppers on, Angela, yours or his?"

I chuckled, grabbed the wheelchair, and pushed Uncle Charlie out before they could get into another silly altercation. I knew they'd both forget what they had been fighting about in five minutes.

We took a table in the back and I went to the bar for a pitcher of diet soda and a couple of glasses. When I got back, my uncle took one look at the pitcher, grimaced at my choice, then poured.

I looked at him affectionately. He was still a handsome man despite his age and the fact that he had had severe diabetes. He had thick dark hair, a powerful chest and arms, and was still pretty fit despite the loss of his legs. And Uncle Charlie still had his wits about him, unlike some of his drinking pals. True, he had a bit of a ruddy complexion from his early days of drinking. Of course, I suspected that he still had the occasional bottle of beer or glass of red wine with his buddies, but when asked about it, he would vehemently deny going off his diet.

"So how's your mother, Angie?" He took a sip of diet soda and made a face, muttering, "It just isn't the same without the sugar."

I ignored his comment and shrugged, then addressed his question. "I didn't get out to her house for dinner last week. I'll try to get down there this Sunday."

He laughed. "I'll bet she wasn't happy to hear your excuse."

I grinned and replied, "I didn't make the excuse. Rosa did."

My uncle let out a guffaw and said, "Poor little Rosa. What did she tell Rosetta?"

My mother's name is Rosetta, as in the Stone. Rosetta Anna Matelli. It's quite a mouthful. We were just thankful that none of us girls were named after her.

"Rosa told Ma I was working on a big important case and couldn't get away."

"Was it a lie?"

I shrugged. "At the time, I guess it wasn't exactly the truth. But I am working on Tom Grady's death."

He sobered. "Don't let your work consume you, Angie. Someday you'll appreciate having a family. Don't turn your back on us yet."

I grinned, reached for his hand, and gave it a squeeze. "I promise to be a good Italian girl when this case is over. I'll go every Sunday to Ma's for dinner for an entire month."

He turned back to the subject of why we were meeting.

"So tell me more, Angie. Have the police closed the case yet?"

"I have a connection in the precinct who tells me that the case is unofficially closed. There wasn't enough evidence to link a suspect to Tom Grady's death. I think they've already written it off as a random killing that just happened to take the life of an ex-police officer."

Our pizza arrived after a while and I realized how hungry I was. Uncle Charlie and I ate in silence for the next few minutes.

"This isn't half bad," he said through a mouthful of vegetarian pizza.

When we'd slowed down, he said, "Okay, kid. We've talked a little about the case. I know you've got something for me."

I took the notebook out of my jacket pocket and handed it to him, explaining how it came into my possession. By the end of my account of hiding under the bed while two Irish thugs searched the bedroom, my uncle's eyes were as wide as my nieces' and nephews' eyes on Christmas morning.

He took his reading glasses out of his jacket pocket, put them on, then inspected the pages. "These are written in Tommy's hand, all right. I've had to decipher enough of these."

I said, "Can you read it?"

Uncle Charlie peered at the first page. "Not enough light in this place." He looked up at me and said, "Mind if I take this home? I can have it back to you by tomorrow."

I felt a little impatient, but realized that he needed some time to study it. I leaned forward and said, "That's fine, but is there anything there that you can give me right now?"

He stopped at one page and stared at it, then handed it to me to read. "There's a name here. James Kersh?" He looked up at me expectantly.

I frowned. "Does it mean anything to you?"

He shook his head. "Not a thing. If he's a crook mixed up in Tommy's death, he must be small-time. It may have been a few years since I retired, but if he was a big troublemaker, I'd remember."

This was really the first time I'd looked carefully at one of the pages. It took me a moment to see the name among all the gibberish. No wonder I hadn't seen it when I'd gone through the notebook a few hours ago. I'd only given the pages a cursory glance. James Kersh. The name hadn't come up in the investigation. I wondered if Kersh had some connection with Brian Scanlon or Seamus McRaney. The name didn't sound Gaelic, but you can never tell. I handed it back after memorizing the name. My uncle pocketed the notebook pages. I picked up the check for dinner.

"You can legitimately write this one off as a business expense," Uncle Charlie gallantly explained. "It would just cut into my measly pension."

*Measly pension, hah,* I thought. My uncle was doing very well. Just after retirement, before he went into the hospital, the price of East Boston property went up. "No-Legs" Charlie owned quite a few choice waterfront properties. And he was no fool—he sold them for a tidy sum, enough for him to retire to the south of Italy, if that was his pleasure. But there was still enough "Old Country" conventions inbred in my uncle for him to feel the ties of family, friends, and East Boston.

I wheeled him out the door and we parted, Uncle Charlie heading up Maverick Street to his townhouse on New Street. I went back to my apartment on Marginal Street.

# ♣ Chapter 18

It was only two in the afternoon when I got home. My answering machine had two messages on it. Both were from my mother. Counting yesterday's message, that was three and I was beginning to feel guilty for putting off calling her, so I dialed.

"So you finally got around to returning my call, Miss Big-Time Private Detective," she said.

"Sorry, Ma," I said, wincing into the phone. "I've been busy." The excuse sounded lame even to me. "Look, I'm on this case and have run into some snags—"

"You're all right, aren't you?" Ma asked anxiously, interrupting my explanation. "I mean, you're not getting beat up or having to resort to guns like they do in the movies, right?"

I sighed. "No, Ma. Nothing like that. It's just a routine little murder case."

"Murder?" she asked, her tone sharp. "As in that nice Mr. Grady, Charlie's friend?"

"How do you know about that? You live in Malden."

"Believe it or not, Angie, we get the *Boston Globe* here, too. I don't live out in the sticks, you know."

"Oh." I always equated Malden with the sticks.

"You *are* coming for dinner tomorrow night, aren't you?" It wasn't a question, it was a summons.

"I'll try, Ma. I really will."

Silence on her end of the line. I began to get nervous.

"Honestly, Ma. It's just that this case is finally starting to come together and . . ." I'd run out of excuses, so I repeated my sincere tone again. "I'll really try, Ma. Honest."

Her tone softened, indicating that she had won this round of verbal sparring. "You're a good girl, Angie, but sometimes I think you got no respect for family."

"What do you mean, no respect?" My temper flared like a dam bursting. All reason flies out the window when one of the Matellis gets mad. "Who brought you to the hospital when you had that stroke? Who stayed by your bed day and night, waiting for you to recover?" I found myself genuflecting automatically. You can take the girl out of Catholicism, but you can never take Catholicism out of the girl.

"Don't start with me, Angela Agnes," she countered. "I nursed you through pneumonia, measles, and mumps when you were little." Another skirmish, this time using our mutual history of sickness and disease as weapons.

"You exposed me to the mumps," I yelled. "I wouldn't have had to spend a week in bed with the mumps if you hadn't dragged me in to play with Sophia."

"Sophia had mumps, and back then our doctors were advising us to expose our children to the measles and the mumps to build up immunity," she replied in her very sensible tone. "I only did it for your benefit, Angela."

My anger dried up like a puddle of water on a hot day. "Yeah, you did your best, Ma," I said, then sighed. "I know that. But please don't pull these guilt trips with me about Sunday dinners. I know you want the family there, and I try to accommodate you. But it doesn't always work out. I have to make a living first."

I heard her sniffle on the other end of the line. *Oh, boy, here come the tears,* I thought.

"I know," Ma said in a tight voice. "But sometimes I feel like I'm losing my children. You're all drifting away from me."

"I'll try to be there, Ma," I repeated. "And I'll see if Rosa can make it, too."

The rest of the phone call included a running commentary on the health of the Matellis, second cousins included. I vaguely remember words like *hysterectomy, prostate problems,* and *asthma* were mentioned, along with other indelicate medical terms. After we'd hung up, I realized that I was depressed.

I made myself a glass of iced tea and thought about the name in the notebook, James Kersh. Maybe it was time to call Craig Cohen again. There was a slim chance he could answer my question. I dialed and let the phone ring. He picked it up on the fifth ring.

"Craig Cohen here," he answered, as tersely as if he were in the office.

"It's Angela. I got another name for you. You don't have to do much research right now, but does the name James Kersh ring any bells?"

"Yeah, I knew him."

"Knew him?"

"Yeah, he was a freelance reporter who worked for us occasionally."

"You're talking in the past tense," I said, a feeling of dread coming over me. "What happened to him?"

Craig replied, "He was killed over a week ago in Haymarket."

A chill ran through me. "How was he killed?"

"Knifed," Craig replied. "Supposed to have been a mugger."

"Maybe this is all coincidence," I said slowly, "but two weeks ago was the day I opened my agency. On my way to work that morning, I walked by the scene of a knifing in Haymarket Square."

"That must have been Kersh," Craig replied.

"Are you thinking what I'm thinking?" I asked.

"The M.O. was the same as for Tom Grady's murder," he replied thoughtfully. "But lots of people are mugged and knifed in Boston," he argued, then amended, "Well, relatively speaking. What I mean is that we can't jump to the conclusion that this is a conspiracy."

"But in this case, there might be a connection. Tell me, do you know what Kersh was working on?"

"Not specifically. He wrote stories with an international slant. He considered himself a real hotshot reporter."

I hesitated, then said, "There's something I haven't told you yet." I paused, then continued, "About two hours before Grady was mugged and killed in the Combat Zone, I was attacked by a mugger with a knife, near Faneuil Hall."

Craig was silent on the other end. He finally said, "Be careful, Angie. Don't do anything stupid. If there is a connection, someone out there knows who you are. It could get you hurt."

"I appreciate your concern, Craig," I replied, "but I have a job to do."

I knew that I had only one, maybe two more days before I was officially off the case. I had to find Eileen tonight. I had to go to the Combat Zone, but I wasn't going to tell Craig Cohen that. After assuring him that I would be careful, we hung up.

It was about seven in the evening when I walked out of my apartment. I noticed that Sophia had been here. Several carry-out pizza cartons were propped up against the wall outside the first-floor apartment door.

I headed for the Zone. I got to the Exchange around eight o'clock, and I found Eileen at a table with some of her pals. I caught her eye and she excused herself from the group.

We found some decent light near the end of the bar and huddled there. "I have some photos here that I'd like you to take a look at," I said, taking the sheaf of pictures from my bag and handing them to her.

She studied them one by one, chewing on her lip pensively, and said, "Well, I can't be certain, but this guy looks familiar. I may have just seen him around the Zone. It's so hard to give you a definite answer." She pointed to Running Shoes, Liam O'Kelly. I was a little surprised. Although I hadn't met either man personally, Eammon O'Driscoll seemed to be more the type to do physical harm. He was big, muscular and, from my viewpoint under Grady's bed a few days ago, Eammon appeared to be more at ease with breaking the law. It was all the more apparent to me since Craig had told me that O'Driscoll was familiar with explosives.

I thanked her and let her go back to her friends.

"Hope you catch whoever did it," she called over her shoulder.

It seemed a little crass to tell Eileen that I hoped her sex change operation went well and that she got out of the drug business, so I settled for a friendly wave.

While I was out and about, I decided it wouldn't hurt to go to dinner and maybe catch a movie. I ate Chinese, then caught a second-run film in a theater off the Common near Arlington Street.

When the film ended, I caught the T back to Maverick and walked home. My mind was abuzz with thoughts of the movie as I approached my building, so it didn't immediately register that the light in the hall entrance wasn't on. When I pushed the front door open and stepped inside, he came out from the shadows of the stairwell. Before I had time to react, something was slipped around my throat and pulled tight. I dropped my shoulder bag and grabbed at the cord instinctively with one hand, thrashing my free arm out in an effort to get him off balance. He pulled the cord tighter. I felt as if all my blood vessels were going to explode. The worst part was that I couldn't scream.

Through the pounding of rushing blood, I heard him whisper, "I warned you." The malevolent tone would have made me shudder if I hadn't been fighting for my life.

I threw my body weight against him, hoping he'd bang into a wall and let up on the pressure he was applying to strangling me, but he was stronger than I'd estimated.

My chest began to burn from lack of air. This was the end. I'd die in this hallway, two floors below my apartment, a floor below Rosa's apartment. I couldn't scream to summon help or warn her. I began to fear that she'd interrupt this scene and be hurt herself. Then I started to lose consciousness.

There was a bang, a rustling sound, a thud, and a clank. Then came an ear-piercing screech.

"Get the hell out of here," I heard someone scream. The pressure on my throat let up and I collapsed on the floor, gasping for air. I must have blacked out for a while. When I opened my eyes, I saw an orange right by my nose. I groaned and reached up to my throat, which was sore both inside and out.

"What the hell—" I managed to croak.

Sophia came over. "Are you all right?"

I got up and stared at the vegetables, the cartons of eggs and milk, and the jar of peanut butter scattered all over the floor of the hallway. "What's all this?"

"My groceries. You owe me a dozen eggs and some milk for saving your miserable life," my sister replied, obviously very concerned for my welfare. "What the hell is going on in this place? How much do you owe the mob? Geez, Angie, they play pretty rough sometimes."

It was hard for me to laugh, but I couldn't help it. Sophia thinks everyone in trouble owes the mob. My voice was little more than a whisper, but I managed to thank her with a hug.

"The first month's rent is free," I said in a rare moment of generosity. I knew I'd regret it later. "If I'd been you, I would have turned around and looked for help. How did you manage to scare him off like that?"

She grinned and shrugged. "I have to handle those types at work all the time. They don't scare me easy. I just grabbed the first thing I could get my hands on and started whacking him over the head with it until he'd had enough." She held up a salami.

We both had a good laugh. Then she turned serious. "What the hell is going on, Angie? I'm concerned about you, but also concerned about moving Michael and Stephanie in here. Does this kind of thing happen all the time?"

"No, Sophia," I rasped, "this was definitely a rare occurrence."

With the help of the banister, I pulled myself up to a standing position. I took three steps outside and stumbled. My vision hadn't cleared yet and nothing was working right. Once I'd sucked in enough fresh night air, once the oxygen had infiltrated my brain again, I peered around Marginal Street in search of my attacker. There wasn't a soul out on the road. I turned back and went inside. The hall light was on again. Sophia was still standing there, pale and trembling.

"You didn't happen to get a look at him . . ." I asked,

trailing off as my sister shook her head.

"It was too dark," she replied.

I sighed. "I didn't think so."

She helped me up the stairs and opened the door to my apartment, an unusually maternal gesture for Sophia. After seeing me inside, she looked around and said, "You know, I could do a lot with this place—"

I made a face and we started laughing hysterically again. I don't think I've ever felt closer to my older sister.

## ♣ Chapter 19

*I* slept like a log that night. It was almost ten o'clock when I woke up the next morning. I must have needed the sleep. Turning off the phone and letting the answering machine take all incoming calls was a great help. It had a twofold purpose: I could get the sleep needed, and if Sheilah, Brian, or the mysterious caller dialed my number, I wouldn't have to deal with them.

I padded into the bathroom. Looking in the mirror, I inspected the burns from the cord and rubbed some cream and antiseptic on my neck. After puttering around the apartment for an hour getting ready for the day, I called Uncle Charlie.

My throat still felt raw both inside and out from my little workout last night, so I had to talk softly. "So what's the news on the notebook, Uncle Charlie?"

"You sound sick, Angie," my uncle replied, his voice full of concern. "You gettin' a cold or something?"

"It's nothing. I've just got a little frog in my throat," I whispered. "So what's up?"

"Angie," he said sternly, "if I'd known the truth, I wouldn't have sent Tommy to you."

"Uncle Charlie, I don't have time for this. Please tell me what was in the notebook."

"According to his notes," he said, "ILAP is a front for an offshoot of the IRA called the Soldiers of Destiny. ILAP was designed to get money from wealthy Irish-Americans for SoD's agenda."

"Big surprise," I replied. "So while these generous Irish-Americans believe they are helping the widows and orphans of Belfast, the old country, ILAP is funneling the funds into the Soldiers of Destiny's paramilitary activities such as buying bombs and guns."

"You've got it," he replied. "This is a full-scale operation. Do you know how the Soldiers of Destiny get the guns?"

"Don't tell me," I said dryly. "Let me guess. Brian Scanlon is their contact."

"Well, he does have a record for this sort of thing," Uncle Charlie admitted. "Have you found out who James Kersh is, or do I have to tell you?"

I sighed. "I talked to a reporter friend last night and he gave me the lowdown. Kersh was a reporter who had a big interest in international issues, especially the IRA."

Uncle Charlie filled me in on the rest. "Kersh was working on exposing the whole scam, once he'd gotten enough evidence. He'd been following McRaney for weeks, snapping photos of the people McRaney met with. But something went wrong near Haymarket. Someone must have spotted him. Maybe Kersh got pictures of some illegal transaction."

"And the film was never found?" I asked.

"Not the film or the camera," he replied.

I thought back to the Haymarket crime scene of two weeks ago. I didn't recall seeing a camera near his body. Maybe the crime scene unit got it, but I doubted it.

"But there's no proof for any of this," I said, my shoulders slumping. "Most of this was stuff I suspected already, and Grady knew it, but now he's dead. I don't suppose there's anything in that notebook that points to some concrete evidence."

"No, but there's some information here that you may not know yet. Maybe it will help you put your case in perspective." Then Uncle Charlie told me that Grady's notes included a warning about plans for a bomb that would be planted during a large gathering.

A few days ago, I'd seen McRaney and his two IRA thugs reading the account of the bombing in Dublin. And Eammon O'Driscoll was good with a fuse. I should have figured this out a long time ago. At least I was now putting two and two together and coming up with four: Brian Scanlon, Eammon O'Driscoll, Seamus McRaney, and, although I had yet to discover his talents, Liam O'Kelly.

Uncle Charlie also told me something that surprised me—Sheilah was an active member of the IRA and an even more active member of the Soldiers of Destiny. No wonder someone was trying to extinguish my lights. If I hadn't been so close to the situation, I might have noticed sooner. I guess my two and two now made five instead of four.

"Look, Uncle Charlie," I said, "something happened last night that makes me leery of picking up that notebook."

"Do you want me to hang on to it?" my uncle responded.

I knew Randolph should have it as soon as possible.

"Can you deliver it to Detective Lee Randolph today?" I told my uncle which precinct.

"Yeah, sure. I can get it to him." My uncle paused, then said, "You all right, Angie?"

"Yeah. Why?"

"I'm just worried that you're in over your head on this one." He added, "You know, I still got some pals on the force. You just say the word and I'll call 'em up for you. You might want to hand this one over to someone else now that it's turned hot."

I laughed hoarsely. "Thanks, Uncle, but I don't think there's enough proof yet. I want to dig a little more. But I promise to turn this over to the police if I haven't gotten anywhere by tomorrow. I'd appreciate it if you'd do that little errand for me."

"No problem. Will Randolph be there on the weekend?"

"If he isn't, just leave it with the desk sergeant. I'll try to reach Randolph after we hang up and I'll be sure to mention that you're bringing it, along with your transcription of the notes."

I thanked my uncle again and we hung up.

Now that I knew the truth, I had to reach Randolph. I called his office number, hoping he'd be there on a Sunday, trying to catch up on his workload. Instead, I got the desk sergeant.

"You wanna leave a message or somethin'?" he asked.

"I don't suppose you could give me his home phone," I asked, adding quickly, "This is an emergency."

The desk sergeant sighed wearily and replied, "It's always an emergency, lady. That's why we got other detectives who're on duty on the weekend. I can get you one of them."

Frustrated, I hung up. I picked up the receiver again and dialed Sheilah and Brian's number. I let it ring twenty times, just to make sure. No one answered.

Next, I punched in the number for ILAP. Ten rings later, a very harried voice answered. It sounded like Bit, but I didn't take the time to find out.

"Is Sheilah Grady there, by any chance?"

"No," the voice answered shortly, "she's at MIT. She'll be there all day for the rally."

I thanked the voice on the other end and hung up. This would be a perfect time to do a little more research—in Chelsea. When I got outside, I noticed that the weather was warming up. As I started my car, a light rain coated the windshield.

I drove to Brian and Sheilah's place in record time—under fifteen minutes. The townhouse had no sign of life in it. I peeked through the narrow rectangular windows of the garage. There was no car there, either. They had apparently taken both cars.

I went to the front door and rang the doorbell. After a few minutes, I decided to let myself in. I'd thought terrorists would have better locks on their doors, but I found it surprisingly easy to break into their place. A credit card did the trick. I slid my rectangle of plastic through the crack and jiggled it until the flimsy latch slipped free.

I stepped inside and closed the door silently behind me. The house had the same empty feeling as Grady's place. I started prowling around. The townhouse felt so temporary. The furniture was bland and modern, the type that was sometimes used in showcase homes in developments. There wasn't an ounce of personality in the living room, dining room, or kitchen.

I climbed the stairs, careful to check out every detail, then went through two more featureless rooms—one had obviously been used as an office, the other was a second bedroom. The master bedroom was just as dull, but with one interesting feature: Half of the drawers and half the closet space were empty. I noted that there were no suitcases stored anywhere, which was a pretty good indication of the line along which I was thinking. Next, I checked the bathroom and found no razors, no shaving cream, and only one toothbrush.

It didn't take a genius to figure out that Brian had packed up for a long trip. Grady's notebook had mentioned that a bomb would be set to go off in a large gathering. There was no reference to when or where. But the absence of Scanlon's things must mean that it was going off today. And there was a large rally at MIT's Briggs Field this afternoon.

Why wasn't Sheilah going with him? I asked myself. My answer was that she wasn't an ex-con and it was less likely that she would be suspected. And she still had to sell her father's house and belongings before going underground. They must have counted on the fact that there was nothing to connect her to her father's death.

It was then that I realized the only person who could connect it all together was me, at least until the notebook fell into Randolph's hands. They had killed James Kersh and Tom Grady. They had almost gotten to me a couple of times. If I tried to shoot my big mouth off, I might have an "accident." For all I knew, someone was still following me, watching my every move. A sudden attack of paranoia made me turn around and study the empty bedroom doorway. The Soldiers of Destiny had to be stopped before someone was hurt. Before a lot of people were hurt. My hand was shaking as I reached for the telephone and dialed the police.

The same bored voice as before answered. "Police. What can I do for you?"

"I called before, looking for Detective Randolph," I explained. "Has he called in yet for his messages?"

"No, lady. Not yet. Look, can't this wait till Monday?"

I tapped my foot. "No," I said curtly. "Not if he wants to solve Tom Grady's murder, it can't. Now you get on the phone to him and tell him Angela Matelli called and told him to meet me in Cambridge at the St. Patrick's Day Rally at MIT's Briggs Field. Tell him to get the Cambridge police in on it and they'd better hurry. I'll explain it all to him when I get there in about an hour."

"Wait, let me get this straight—" he started to say. I hung up without waiting for him to start questioning me.

Taking the car to Cambridge was almost as idiotic as walking there from Chelsea, so I decided to take the T. The rain had stopped and the sun was trying to come out. A cool breeze blew in from the nearby bay. I got in my car and drove to an East Boston T station.

The subways were running a little slow on account of the holiday. I saw my share of big, beefy Irish-Americans running around in little green foil hats and green pipe-cleaner shamrock pins. I always figured that St. Patrick's Day was just an excuse for some people to drink green beer and eat corned beef and cabbage, then slap each other on the back and congratulate themselves on being Irish.

I knew who was drunk right away on the subway—if they weren't wearing the hats and pins, they were the guys with bright red noses, telling each other lame leprechaun jokes.

The red line to Alewife was so crowded that I almost missed my stop, Harvard Square. Since there was no direct way of getting to Briggs Field, I figured that I'd catch a taxi to MIT. But as I was emerging from the subway, I caught sight of Sheilah Grady. She was heading for the ILAP offices. I hesitated, wondering whether to go directly to Briggs Field and meet Detective Randolph, or whether to follow Sheilah. I chose to follow her.

The place was almost empty when I got there. There was no sign of Sheilah, but there was one stalwart worker manning the phones. He looked up from his duty and asked, "Do you need directions to the rally? It's going to begin in about fifteen minutes—"

"No, I was just looking for Sheilah Grady and I thought I'd try here before going over to Briggs."

He gestured over his shoulder toward Seamus McRaney's office and said, "Well, you're in luck."

Sheilah breezed out of the office, head down and out of breath. "Jordan, the copy machine's acting up and I need more flyers . . ." She trailed off when she looked up and saw me. Her eyes narrowed and she said, "Brian told you the other night that your services were no longer required."

I looked at Jordan, whose big puppy-dog eyes held a bewildered expression. Then I looked back at Sheilah, wordlessly suggesting that we talk privately. She looked impatiently at her watch.

I said in a grim voice, "This is important, probably more important than your rally." I gestured toward McRaney's office.

She eyed me irritably. "Oh, all right. If you must . . ." Then she stalked into the office, still playing the grudging ingenue. I noticed that the curtains inside the glass wall of the office were only partially closed.

After closing the door, she whirled around and said to me in a fierce tone, "I thought we'd straightened all this out on Friday. Brian fired you. You do not work for me anymore. I certainly hope you haven't been back to my father's house, snooping and prowling around where you don't belong."

I was the picture of innocence as I asked, "What makes you think I was there again?"

She crossed her arms, definitely a hostile gesture. "Brian and I went to Dorchester yesterday afternoon to sort through Daddy's belongings. When I went to the refrigerator to get ice for our sodas, there was water in the ice cube trays."

I dropped the naive act. "Yeah, I was there that morning," I admitted. "And I found something very interesting."

"I'll have you charged with breaking and entering," she shouted, pacing back and forth in an agitated manner.

I smiled calmly and said, "That would be a little hard to prove. Especially since I still have a key to the house."

She stopped pacing and replied, "But you were fired on Friday. You had no right. I'll sue you for violation of privacy."

I shrugged and said, "How was I to know that your boyfriend didn't call up and fire me without your permission? He was pretty angry on Friday when he encountered me with Seamus McRaney. Maybe he persuaded you. Maybe you were under duress when you gave him permission."

"You're fired!" she screeched. "Is that good enough for you? Do I need to type it out and sign it in front of a witness?" She moved around the desk to the typewriter and shoved a paper into it. Then she stabbed a button on the phone and said curtly, "Jordan, I need you in here for a moment."

"I wouldn't do that if I were you," I said quietly.

She ignored me, jabbing the keys viciously. Jordan opened the door and poked his head in. "You need me?" he asked her, eyeing me as if I were an alligator ready to snap at him.

She ripped the page out of the typewriter, a look of triumph on her face, and said, "Yes, I need you to witness my signature, then sign below it."

She signed it with an angry flourish, then watched Jordan bend to the task. A second later, he backed out of the door, leaving it ajar. Sheilah called after him, "Why don't you take a lunch break? I'll take over the phones till you get back."

I heard Jordan mumble his thanks, then the sound of the front door closing. Sheilah made a photocopy of the signed release and handed it to me. Shaking my head, I took it and dropped the house key in her extended palm.

"Your services are now terminated," she said in an icy tone, adding, "Don't bother to send back whatever's left over from the retainer."

With a deep breath, I replied, "Don't worry, I have no intention of sending you anything back. I consider any extra retainer to be payment for aggravation and the expense of learning that my client had a hidden agenda. Besides, you'll be long gone before I could return it anyway."

Her eyes flew open in surprise, then narrowed in suspicion. "What are you talking about?"

"The police don't suspect you of planning your father's murder at the moment, but after you sell the house and slip away, what else can they think?"

"You found his notes," she stated flatly, a dangerous look in her eye. I noticed her hand reaching down into an open desk drawer. I lunged across the desk and slammed the drawer on her fingers. She let out a howl of pain.

I slid off the desk and went around it, grabbing her shoulders and forcing her into the office chair, tilting it back to keep her off balance.

"You think you can get away with murder now?" I asked in a low voice. "Try me. Your dad hired me because I was not only a woman, but an ex-Marine. I can be as tough as the rules call for. Were the proceeds from the house going to help the Soldiers of Destiny, or were you just going to use your inheritance to live on?"

She was shaking now. Beads of sweat appeared on her pale forehead. I grabbed her blazer lapels and pulled her up, roughly turned her around, and pulled one of her arms behind her. I heard a wince of pain escape from her. Then I opened the drawer and found a very nasty-looking Astra .357 automatic.

"So how does it feel to have helped kill your father, Sheilah?" I asked. My voice sounded cold, even to me. "Was I next in line? What were people supposed to think when they found my cold, dead body near Faneuil—that I was mugged like Tom Grady and James Kersh?" She gasped, apparently surprised that I'd put it together. I continued, "And when I didn't die, you made sure that I had a surprise visitor in my apartment building. Is this the price you paid to become a member of the elite—the lives of your father and a reporter?"

She managed to turn her head a bit, then tried to spit in my face. I laughed at her clumsy attempt. An unsure expression crossed her face.

"Why was I hired?" I asked. "You did hire me after the mugging attempt failed. Was it to keep an eye on me?"

"I needed that notebook," she explained between grunts of pain. I was not letting up on my grip. "I'd been through the house several times. Brian and some of the ILAP people had searched it thoroughly, too. No one could find the notes. I found out that he'd hired you. As a cop's daughter, I knew that Dad had evidence that pointed to Brian, Seamus, and ILAP—I knew he'd hidden it somewhere in the house as insurance."

I tugged on her arm again, just for the satisfaction of hearing her discomfort. "Good," I said. "I'm glad it hurts. I hope it hurts more than it apparently hurt you to kill your father." I was starting to scare myself. I had no idea I had this sadistic streak in me. I let up the pressure a bit. Sheilah's free arm came up awkwardly, a stapler in her hand, and before I could react, the edge of the stapler glanced off my temple. I lost my balance and the room spun before my eyes.

I felt Sheilah twist herself out of my grip, turn, and give me the back of her hand. The slap stung my cheek and jaw. I fell back against the printer table, and my hip came in hard contact with one of the metal corners. I heard myself groan.

A smiling Sheilah was standing over me with the .357 automatic. The dizziness wouldn't go away, so I stayed where I was and tried to reason with her.

"Look, Sheilah," I said softly, "if you turn state's evidence and name the killer, you can probably get a reduced sentence."

Tears were streaming down her face. She said, "Do you think it was easy for me to say, 'Okay, go ahead and kill him'? But it had to be done."

I guessed at what had happened. "After you argued with your dad, you made a phone call to Seamus, right?"

Sheilah didn't protest. She continued, "I couldn't let our cause be endangered, not even by my father. I know he was concerned about my involvement with Brian."

"Who called your father," I asked, "Brian or Seamus?"

"Seamus," she replied. "We realized it was the only way to rid ourselves of the problem. Seamus pointed out that I'd inherit the estate, so . . ." She trailed off, sobbing.

I pulled myself slowly up to a more comfortable position on my knees, then said, "It wasn't Seamus who met your father that night, it was Liam, wasn't it?"

"That's right," said another voice from the office door. Liam O'Kelly stood there, a Smith and Wesson .38 in his hand, an even bigger weapon than the Astra. He had a hard look on his face. Now that I could see him up close, I noticed that his eyes were as dead as two stagnant pools. I would have shuddered if I'd been in any shape. But now I knew what Liam's true occupation was—and it wasn't assistant director of ILAP. He was a professional killer.

I felt as if I were going to pass out, but I stayed in a

crouched position. That blow to my head must have whacked something real important.

A sickening taste rose in my throat. I wondered if Randolph was at all concerned, or if he thought I'd just played a very bad practical joke on him.

"Liam!" Sheilah sounded startled and nervous. Her back was to me, but through my veiled sight, I saw her gun hand relax. She said, "I'm relieved that I won't have to do this myself."

"No, you won't," Liam said with a lizardlike smile as he raised his gun and fired a round into Sheilah.

I witnessed her body spasm with the impact of the bullet. Then she slowly turned around to face me and I saw the look of surprise and betrayal on her face as she slid to the floor. I guess Sheilah's last thought was that being a member of the IRA wasn't all it was cracked up to be. I gauged the distance between me and the gun that she'd dropped. Definitely not enough time, but I should at least make the attempt.

I tried to distract him. "So, Liam," I said in as hearty a voice as I could manage, "I suppose you killed James Kersh as well."

"Kersh?" He looked at me sharply. It must have dawned on him suddenly, because he chuckled and replied, "Oh, yes. The reporter. That was a few weeks ago. He didn't put up much of a fight. Spent all his time begging for his life to be spared. He kept telling me he wouldn't say anything to anyone. I never liked sneaks like that. Turn your back to them and they'll take the first opportunity to stab you."

*Like you stabbed both Kersh and Grady,* I thought. But I held my tongue on that one. I wanted to keep him talking, but I didn't want to get him angry at me too early.

I decided to surprise him instead, so I asked, "Tell me, when does that bomb go off and where is it planted?"

Like I had a chance in hell of warning anyone.

Liam looked surprised for a moment, then watched me suspiciously as he replied, "What difference does it make to you? You'll be dead before it's activated."

Where would be a good place for a bomb in Briggs Field? My thoughts raced. Seamus McRaney was supposed to make a speech at the rally. There had to be a raised platform. I took a chance. "It's under the podium, isn't it?"

I had definitely startled him with my guess this time. His eyes darted to the left, then back to me. He raised his gun. I felt my legs cramping, but I stayed crouched.

I talked quickly, trying to keep his attention. "And I'll bet it doesn't go off until you and Eammon and Seamus, and maybe even Brian, are well away from there. You know, that's the problem with terrorists these days. No sense of honor. They're willing to sacrifice everyone's life but their own."

"Shut up!" he said sharply. "I've sacrificed plenty for the cause."

I was on a roll and I intended to stay there, anything to buy some time. "Yeah, you probably sacrificed your parents, siblings, and friends."

For a moment I thought I'd gone too far. His face turned to stone, then he broke into a nasty grin. "You forgot my wife and kids."

I decided to change the subject before my big mouth got me dead faster. "So, Liam," I said, "what's next for you after the bomb goes off? Are you going back to Belfast?"

"There's more work to be done there," he acknowledged. He came farther into the room, walking as sleek and quiet as a cat.

"I suppose you'll have to escape the U.S. through Canada, Mexico, or Miami, right?"

He shrugged. "It won't matter to you."

"I'm curious about one thing," I continued, really reaching now. I moved slowly, planting one foot on the floor. "Was it you who made the threatening phone call to me? And was it you who attacked me both times?"

His eyes narrowed as he thought it over. Finally Liam shrugged. "Well, it won't hurt to tell you now, would it?" he said with a terrible smile. "Curiosity kills and all that, you know."

I shivered as if someone had walked over my grave already, but kept my face composed. Shifting a tiny bit, I planted the other foot on the floor for balance. I wanted to stand up and stretch, but I knew it would probably cost me my life.

"Well, I'll tell you this," he replied. "I attacked you down near Faneuil Hall a few weeks ago. I underestimated your strength and quickness." He eyed me appreciatively and added, "I don't mind tellin' you that if things were different, if you weren't the enemy—" he grinned quickly, not a nice grin, and continued, "I do admire your abilities and your spirit. It's a shame they have to go to waste like this, but—"

I finished for him. "Them's the breaks, as we crass Americans say." I shifted again in an unhurried manner, my poor cramped leg muscles screaming for a nice long stretch.

He seemed to appreciate my wit and chuckled. For a wild moment, I considered trying to convince him that a nice Italian-American girl was interested in joining up with the Soldiers of Destiny. Staring death in the face makes strange bedfellows. I nixed that idea and asked, "What about the phone call and the guy who almost strangled me?"

"Now, the phone call, I can't say for sure, but my guess would be Brian Scanlon. He's been nervous from the beginning about your indirect involvement. He's the only one of us who thought there was more to you than met the eye."

I love being underestimated. I know women are supposed to be insulted by being treated like second-class citizens, but in my profession, it can be an advantage.

"As for last night when you were attacked, that was Eammon. He botched the job, of course. He's used to working with explosives and detonators. It would have been his first hands-on kill. He has the brawn, but apparently not the endurance."

"At least, he doesn't have the stamina to go up against two Matelli women. He ran into my older sister and a salami." My hand automatically went up to my throat. I shifted my position slightly.

Liam looked sharply at my movements, but relaxed when he realized I was remembering last night's attack. "So Eammon was chased away by another woman, eh? That's not the way he tells it. He told me two men walked in on the job."

I tried to laugh. "Well, I guess that's something you can use against him sometime."

"Aye," he said, pointing his weapon at me. So much for the psychology of talking to your attacker on a personal level to convince him not to kill you.

I attempted a smile and said, "I don't suppose you can just tie me up and leave me here to explain away all of this."

"No, that I cannot do," he replied confidently, getting ready to squeeze the trigger.

During our little discussion, I had been slowly pulling myself upright into a crouch, little by little. My only chance was to go for the Astra that lay next to Sheilah's dead body. I had nothing to lose, so I sprang and rolled.

I heard the sound of gunfire, but wasn't hit. Reaching

my goal, I grabbed the automatic and in one beautiful, fluid movement ended up in a crouched position, ready for action.

I was congratulating myself on a feat that went beyond the Olympics when I looked up, gun in hand, and saw Liam's jaw go slack and his knees buckle. He fell down dead at my feet.

Behind him, Brian Scanlon stood with a smoking gun in his hand. He was staring in horror at Sheilah's crumpled and bloody body. Tears rolled unabashedly down his face. I got the feeling that he wasn't even aware that I was in the room.

I aimed my gun at him and said gently, "Drop it, Brian. I'm very familiar with guns and won't hesitate to use it."

He complied reluctantly and put down the gun.

"Brian, I understand why Tom Grady was killed," I said. "But why the bomb? Why hurt and kill hundreds of innocent people here in the States? The war is thousands of miles away."

He smiled without warmth, his eyes still fastened on Sheilah's body. All the fight had gone out of him, all the anger toward me had vanished. "We wanted to bring the horror of what was happening in Northern Ireland here to Boston," he explained wearily. "So all the Irish-Americans drinking their green beer on St. Patrick's Day would get a taste of the reality Seamus and his people live with every day in Belfast."

Brian turned toward me and asked, "Can I go to her?"

I nodded silently. He walked over, knelt down, and cradled her in his arms. "I loved her, you know," he said softly to no one in particular. Unless I counted.

With my eye still on him, I picked up the phone and dialed 911. Detective Lee Randolph arrived within minutes. He stood in the doorway with a couple of uniformed Cambridge officers behind him.

"Jesus," he said, taking in the scene in Seamus's office. "What the hell do you do for an encore, Angie?"

## ♣ *Chapter 20*

s this it, or do you have more to tell me?" Randolph asked, letting the uniformed police into the office to take Brian Scanlon into custody and seal off the crime scene.

I was gently guided out of Seamus's office by one of the officers. Suddenly bone-tired and aching all over, I shook my head in answer to Randolph's question.

I managed to reply, "How about stopping a bomb from going off under the podium at MIT's Briggs Field?"

I started to head for the door, but he grabbed my arm. "Hold on, Angie," Randolph said. "Can you take a moment to let me in on what's happening? If I'm going to make an arrest, I'd like to know what's going down."

I was impatient to get to Briggs Field. "Let's talk on the way."

I emerged from the ILAP offices to find that the day had gotten warmer. An ambulance was double-parked outside and paramedics were getting stretchers ready.

Randolph paused, peered at me, and said, "Are you all right? Maybe I should have one of these guys check you out."

I shook my head. "Thanks, but I'm fine. I've got to see this thing through."

He nodded. "Let's go."

We got into his unmarked car and drove toward Briggs Field via Mass Ave. Randolph thought it would be faster than trying to come in along the north side of the field by Vassar Avenue. Cars and people attending the rally would be clogging up Vassar.

I gave Randolph the Cliff Notes version of the results of my investigation. When I was finished, he looked over at me, a tight expression on his face. "You should have waited for me before coming down here," he finally said. "All this killing might have been avoided."

I shrugged. "If I'd come to you with what I'd had before this, would you have believed me?"

He glanced away for a moment to contain his temper. "It was still a pretty stupid thing for you to do," he replied. I guess that was as close as he was going to get to admitting that I was right.

As we approached MIT, Randolph radioed the Cambridge police for backup and a bomb squad. There were cars parked along Mass Ave near Briggs Field, some squeezing into impossibly small spaces, some into illegal spaces. Randolph double-parked and we got out of the car. As we headed for the field, we first had to pass the plaza in front of the MIT Student Union, which was thick with students, teachers, and other politically active people. Randolph elbowed our way through the milling crowd until we finally reached the edge of the field.

I could hear Seamus McRaney's Irish lilt over the tinny loudspeakers. I was pretty sure that the bomb wouldn't be detonated until the fearless leader of the International League for the Advancement of Peace was safely out of harm's way. It was all right to sacrifice innocent bystanders, but the chief always had to remain safe, far away from the violence.

We reached the podium just as Seamus McRaney was

winding up his speech. I could hear the wail of sirens in the distance. Looking up at McRaney, I could see that he had heard the squad cars as well. His eyes had begun to search the crowd. *He's looking for Liam,* I thought.

Randolph turned to me and said, "Is there anyone else who needs to be taken in for questioning?"

I spotted a nervous-looking Eammon O'Driscoll near the stands and pointed him out to Detective Randolph. "He's the demolitions expert," I explained. "He also assaulted me in the hallway of my building, if that counts for anything."

Randolph raised his eyebrows in response and replied, "Then I guess you'll need to make a statement downtown if you're going to press charges." We looked at each other and grinned. Chalk up one more charge to keep the riffraff in jail where they belong.

Two uniformed officers came toward us. Randolph leaned over and gave them instructions, pointing out Eammon O'Driscoll. I watched them circle him like two vultures looking for some fresh meat. When they had him in custody, Randolph and I waited by the raised platform where Seamus McRaney stood, listening to his final words.

". . . And I'd just like to thank all the courageous Irish-Americans who believe in freedom for the world over. God bless you for your contributions, and happy St. Paddy's Day!" Seamus stepped off the podium amid a burst of enthusiastic applause. Although he was standing only three feet away from me, he didn't see me right away.

"Oh, for Christ's sake, Seamus," I said in his ear. "Happy St. Paddy's Day? I'll bet it's barely acknowledged as a holiday in the old country. Couldn't you do better than that?"

Seamus stiffened at the sound of my voice. Then he

turned around to face me, a smile pasted on his face.

"Why, Angela Matelli! It certainly is a surprise to see you here. I thought you were Italian."

"Italian, Irish, what does it matter?" I replied airily. "The United States *is* the melting pot, you know."

"Aye," he said, giving me a charming smile. "It's known the world over."

"And I guess this place is going to be a literal melting pot in a few minutes," I said, crossing my arms casually.

"Whatever do you mean by that?" he said, looking at his watch.

I clamped a hand on his arm and asked, "Oh, am I keeping you from a pressing engagement?"

"Well, actually, I do have some plans," Seamus said, starting to edge away from me. I kept a firm hold on his arm. He glanced back at the empty podium.

I gave him my brightest smile and said sweetly, "By the way, may I introduce Detective Lee Randolph? He's with Homicide." Randolph stepped up, a stern look on his face. Then I pointed in the distance and added, "And here come the boys from the bomb squad."

Randolph collared McRaney and took out his handcuffs. While slapping the metal bracelets on McRaney, he recited in a cheery voice, "You have the right to remain silent. Anything you say may be used against you in a court of law. . . ."

As Randolph finished reading Miranda to him, McRaney went limp. Just before he was taken away, Seamus paused, looked at me, and said with confidence, "I won't be charged, you know. No one will say a word against me. Not Liam, not Eammon, not Sheilah, not Brian."

He was right about Liam and Sheilah—they were dead. And he was probably right about Eammon as well. But I wouldn't bet money on all of his prediction:

Seamus McRaney, intrepid leader of the Soldiers of Destiny, did not yet know that Brian Scanlon was one unhappy boy right now. Brian had loved Sheilah and she had died not at the hands of the enemy, but at the hands of people who Brian and Sheilah had considered their comrades. By now, Brian had had enough time to place some of the blame. And I had a feeling that his girlfriend's death would be placed squarely on Seamus's shoulders.

"I don't know if I would sound so sure of myself," I replied, "until I knew all of the facts."

Seamus shook his head and said, "They won't talk. They all know how important the cause is. I won't do a day of time."

A policeman escorted Seamus McRaney to a waiting squad car and shoved him inside, making sure the founder of ILAP didn't hit his head. Seamus looked back at me, a triumphant smile on his face. I smiled back.

I sat in my office, glad to have my lunch break. Piles of insurance and repo forms were scattered all over my desk. I made a mental note to pick up a couple of those desk organizers so I can stack it all up in one corner of the desk. My sandwich sat in front of me, uneaten. Three empty coffee cups were lined up on the left side of my desk and a fourth one, half full and lukewarm, was in front of me.

It had been almost a week since Brian, Seamus, and Eammon were taken into custody. The crowd had dispersed with a minimum of panic and the bomb squad had arrived to dismantle the bomb with twenty minutes left on the clock. I guess Seamus and the gang wanted to be sure that they were well away when it went off.

I went down to headquarters the next day and gave my statement. Uncle Charlie had delivered Tom Grady's notes which were now being held as evidence for the murder trial. Randolph told me that Seamus was quite surprised to hear about Liam's death, but he didn't seem surprised that Sheilah was dead. I wondered privately if, before they blew town, Seamus, Liam, and Eammon had planned all along to get rid of Sheilah and Brian just to wrap everything up neatly. I guess I would never know.

But I did know that Eammon and Seamus would be put away for a long time. Brian, no longer a leader but a follower, was talking, naming names, dates, times, everything. And he'd brought down the previously untouchable Seamus McRaney.

There had been some publicity on the arrest of the IRA members, and I had gotten a modest mention in connection with solving the case. It had been a boost to my business. Bob Leone had called me about more work with insurance claims, and a credit company contacted me yesterday about taking care of a few repossessions. I was doing pretty well for a private investigator who had been in business less than a month.

The phone rang now and I eagerly picked it up, expecting the call to be another client. I'd finally settled on how I'd answer the phone.

"Matelli Investigations," I said smoothly.

"Angie. It's your mother," said the voice on the other end of the line. "It's been three weeks since I've seen you. You *are* coming down this week for Sunday dinner, aren't you?"

My shoulders caved in.

"Yes, Ma," I said, the whine apparent in my voice. I winced. "I'll be there. I promise this time I'll be there."

# Build yourself a library of paperback mysteries to die for—DEAD LETTER

**NINE LIVES TO MURDER** by Marian Babson
When actor Winstanley Fortescue takes a nasty fall—or was he pushed?—he finds himself trapped in the body of Monty, the backstage cat.
_____ 95580-4 ($4.99 U.S.)

**THE BRIDLED GROOM** by J. S. Borthwick
While planning their wedding, Sarah and Alex—a Nick and Nora Charles of the 90's—must solve a mystery at the High Hope horse farm.
_____ 95505-7 ($4.99 U.S./$5.99 Can.)

**THE FAMOUS DAR MURDER MYSTERY**
by Graham Landrum
The search for the grave of a Revolutionary War soldier takes a bizarre turn when the ladies of the DAR stumble on a modern-day corpse.
_____ 95568-5 ($4.50 U.S./$5.50 Can.)

**COYOTE WIND** by Peter Bowen
Gabriel Du Pré, a French-Indian fiddle player and part-time deputy, investigates a murder in the state of mind called Montana.
_____ 95601-0 ($4.50 U.S./$5.50 Can.)

THE SARAH DEANE MYSTERIES BY

 **J. S. BORTHWICK**

FROM ST. MARTIN'S PAPERBACKS
—COLLECT THEM ALL!

# BODIES OF WATER
_____ 92603-0   $4.50 U.S./$5.50 Can.

# THE CASE OF THE HOOK-BILLED KITES
_____ 92604-9   $4.50 U.S./$5.50 Can.

# THE DOWN EAST MURDERS
_____ 92606-5   $4.50 U.S./$5.50 Can.

# THE STUDENT BODY
_____ 92605-7   $4.50 U.S./$5.50 Can.

# THE BRIDLED GROOM
_____ 95505-7   $4.99 U.S./$5.99 Can.

As storm clouds gather over Europe and FDR receives such guests as Albert Einstein, Joe Kennedy and crime buster Eliot Ness, Eleanor is thrust into danger much closer to home. One of the President's staff has been found dead, poisoned by cyanide mixed in his evening bourbon. Even worse, the accused killer is another White house aide, diminutive beauty Thérèse Rolland.

Although the police are determined to pin the crime on Thérèse, Eleanor is immediately convinced she is innocent. Calmly, but firmly, the First Lady uncovers a web of lies and secrets swirling around the Louisiana political machine...until another shocking murder is discovered. Suddenly, the investigation is taking Eleanor Roosevelt places no proper First Lady would ever go—to the darkest underside of society, and toward a shattering truth that lies within the White House itself!

ELLIOTT ROOSEVELT

# MURDER IN THE WEST WING

### An Eleanor Roosevelt Mystery

### "Compelling!" —*Kirkus*